For Willa

Barbara Ken Davis

LETTERS TO MY HUSBAND'S ANALYST

Letters to My Husband's Analyst

<<<<<<<<<<<<<< >>>>>>>>>>>>>

BARBARA KERR DAVIS

HAWTHORN BOOKS, INC.
Publishers/NEW YORK
A Howard & Wyndham Company

The quotation on pages 79 and 80 is from *Under the Net* by Iris Murdoch. Published by Penguin Books © 1954 by Iris Murdoch. Used by permission.

The poem quoted on page 119 is from "Cinderella" in *Transformations* by Anne Sexton. Published by Houghton Mifflin Company © 1971 by Anne Sexton. Used by perimssion.

LETTERS TO MY HUSBAND'S ANALYST

Library of Congress Catalog Card Number: 78–65408
ISBN: 0–8015–4518–8

1 2 3 4 5 6 7 8 9 10

Part One

October 12

Dear Dr. Frickman,

I probably shouldn't be writing. I mean, I don't know too much about psychoanalysis. Or rather, I didn't until Jake started seeing you ten months ago. (I've been doing a bit of reading up since then.) But I know enough now to know that you analysts have lots of little in-group rules, that you have your own holy, inner-sanctum type of secrets that you keep from us laymen—or laywoman, in my case— and that a lot of things can interfere with the process of analysis. Which is the last thing I want to do, since Jake is (or at least was) so enthused about seeing you. (Naturally he calls you a prick sometimes, but that's all part of the process, right?)

Anyway, in case you're wondering why in the world I'm writing to you, it's because, quite frankly, you have become a third party in our marriage, and I feel it's unfair that I should be left out of analysis. You're getting a nice sum of money (though let me now express gratitude for the reduced fee), which rightfully belongs to me—or us. So the least you could do is read my side of things. I mean, while Jake is there five mornings a week letting it all hang out, who am I supposed to talk to? And how do I know that what he's telling you isn't a very distorted version of reality? I didn't mind his going to you when he started back in January—I even thought it might be a good idea since he seems so moody sometimes. I didn't even mind the money. At first. But now I'm not sure— especially now that I've read that this can go on for *years*. (Just yesterday I read that Woody Allen's been in for over ten years. Is that true? If it is, that's absurd.) And besides, after all this time, I'm not sure that I really know why Jake felt this great urge to go into analysis. So what is it? What's so wrong with Jake that he needs to see you five mornings a week?

It's sex, isn't it? Is it this twice-a-day desire of his? Or is it that he wants me to mother him—wants to sleep with the mother figure he turns me into? I know a little about your theories, but I can't figure this out. What *is* the problem? We've been married for three years, and I knew Jake for two years before that, so how is it you now know the answer to this expensive question and I don't?

Well, he's in it now and maybe there's no use asking such questions. The whale has swallowed Jonah and I must wait and hope for him to be spewed forth. In the meantime, I do have a more practical reason for writing—and I'm not going to mince words.

It's money. Now I realize that money has a lot of connotations in a relationship between analyst and patient, and of course I respect Jake's need to work through those meanings with you. But I'm wondering if either of you realizes how a little of that money could help our household situation? I'm not asking to get rich—just for you two to be reasonable. I mean, defrosting the tiny freezer inside our antique refrigerator is not one of the joys of my life, but I do have a sense of humor, and I do get a laugh now and then out of chopping at the ice with a kitchen knife. And furniture? I really take a kind of pride in our coffee table, made from a telephone-cable spool, which I caulked and painted canary yellow under the theory that if you can't hide it, accent it; and our secondhand sofa, which I have disinfected and neatly disguised with an Indian print bedspread. I don't even mind living in this semislum apartment building with its dingy hallways and dilapidated stairway. These things I can live comfortably with; we're students, after all, and everyone says we'll look back fondly at all this one day. I'm sure. You see, I'm really not complaining about those kinds of things. But a little more money could sure be put to some good use around here.

Take yesterday, for example. As you probably know, I do substitute teaching and any other part-time jobs I can find on the university bulletin board for the days when I don't have classes myself. Now that Jake's Saturday-job money goes straight to you, I have to supplement the income from my fellowship with these terribly interesting jobs: as a weight-reducing group leader on Tuesday nights (ah: if those chubs only knew I live on chocolate); as a proofreader at a computer information storage company two mornings a week; and, now and then, from selling my body to a drug firm doing research on major tranquilizers, among other things.

Anyway, back to yesterday. After taking two buses and a trolley over to the Kensington section of town, I had to walk three blocks to this really out of the way, graffiti-covered elementary school. Fourth grade, room 211. Substituting is bad enough without getting there late. They make plans while they're waiting for you to arrive. I grew up in a conservative suburban town outside New York, and we thought we were quite bold when we all dropped our books at eleven minutes past two. But here . . . by now I'm only slightly embarrassed by contraceptives used as water-balloons, and I learned long ago how to work the fire extinguisher for "spontaneous" combustion just about anywhere, but yesterday someone urinated on the floor, and the janitor acted so disgusted that he made me feel like I had done it.

The trolley on the way home was filled with kids, so I had to give up reading Sylvia Plath's *Letters Home* (maybe reading all those letters is what prompted me to write to you), and I lost my transfer to the buses and had to pay another thirty-five cents. I didn't have EXACT CHANGE ONLY so I had to give the driver a dollar bill and take a refund slip. This is what Philadelphia, the City of Brotherly Love, has come to—trolley cars that stuff themselves with exact change only. I had a headache when I got home and we didn't even have aspirins in the house, so I knocked on the door just down the hall from us where three guys, all dental students, share an apartment. Michael gave me a whole bottle of aspirins and offered to keep me company while I cooked dinner. I was making my specialty of late, beefed-up biscuit dinner (economical students that we are), which is a combination of hamburger, tomato sauce and quick, refrigerated crescent rolls. (No doubt you have not had the pleasure of beefed-up biscuit, but you know, you might find it a welcome change from steak or roasts or lobster or whatever it is that you and Mrs. Frickman enjoy. Really quite tasty.)

Well, now to the real point I was trying to make. While Michael was sitting at our kitchen table telling me about his problems constructing a partial denture for one clinic patient and complaining about the body odor of another, a pure-bred roach scooted right out from under the table and across the top. Since Michael lives in the next apartment, there was no use treating this as a rare occurrence. They've had the exterminator coming regularly for some time now. But in *our* apartment, Jake insists that we spray for ourselves, that an exterminator's services are too expensive. Now, I could have the exterminator come and really spray well, and keep coming once a month for six months, all for the price of two analytic sessions—just two! And that's only one little example. If I had the money from *one* analytic session to spend on clothes each week, I'd be up next to Jacqueline Onassis on the best-dressed list. A single week's worth of sessions would buy me a one-way ticket to the oblivion of Mardi Gras in New Orleans. Or better yet—and this is a favorite fantasy whenever Jake and I have one of our verging-on-violent disagreements—with less than half the cost of a month's analysis I could rent out a little cottage down the shore with a view of only sand dunes and grass and the sea and sky, where I would surround myself with books, music, tea and Bordeaux cookies and simply study and read and write my dissertation.

Actually, I'm not interested in competing with Jackie or getting lost in New Orleans or even sharing my breakfast with sea gulls and sandpipers just yet. Right now, I'd just like to hire an exterminator. In other words, doctor, in the hopes that you will get the bugs out of my husband's head, I'm living here intimately with other, quite visible bugs. Not that I'm not grateful and hopeful. I'm sure you'll do a fine job—and again, I know that this money question is important between analyst and patient. Just thought I'd put a bug in your ear, as the saying goes.

Sincerely,
MRS. JAKE DANIELS

October 24

DEAR DR. FRICKMAN,

You will no doubt be surprised to receive a second letter from me—and so soon after the first. But I realized, after sending it off, that I had only hit the tip of the iceberg on a problem that I find extremely important. I know that you analysts see almost nothing as accidental, and you may be quite right. It is perhaps quite fitting that the issue I was (too) silent about is silence—yours and Jake's. (Obviously I am *not* silent and I am beginning to feel like a broken record in a Simon and Garfunkel–type "dangling conversation," asking "Can analysis be worthwhile?"—or like a discordant sound amongst the "sounds of silence.") Not that I expect any answer from you, of course. No, I certainly respect the complicated nature of the patient-analyst relationship, the working alliance. (Is that what you call it?) I understand that everything must be quite confidential and that the patient must not know much of anything about the analyst. I'm sure it all makes great therapeutic sense. I am not the patient, and therefore I am not to be included. But *that,* doctor, is what I find difficult to cope with.

After all, you know, I've had something of a working alliance with Jake myself, and for a much longer time. I've been with him for many good times, times that included childishly joyous long rides on the cycle up to the mountains, or spur-of-the-moment adventures riding the Kawasaki across the Walt Whitman Bridge or out to the airport to watch the planes take off for Spain, or France, or who knows where. Alas, poor students dreaming about the great world out there! But I have been drawn into many bad times too. I have long been confidante to those deep Monday-morning depressions when he has had to get up to begin another long week of labs and classes—those cold, still-dark winter mornings when he wraps himself around me and begs for five more minutes of sleep, and then another minute, and another, as if I could make it all go away. I have long shared the Friday- and Saturday-evening sessions (sometimes joined by Michael and Timothy and David, our dental-student neighbors) during which he smokes enough to transport himself to the oblivion of sleep. He's unable to turn off naturally the compulsion that drives him to study until one or two o'clock every night during the week. And the next morning, if I make any reference to it, I'm called a nag—perhaps like his mother, or like the nuns from his early parochial-school years. These and many more moments have I shared for several years with Jake.

And now, doctor, now you have somehow entered into our lives in a manner that can only be called intimate. I suspect that you know how often we make love, or how seldom, and in what manner. I wonder how my tirades about sharing housework are presented in an analytic session. Most of all I wonder about how *you*, how your silent presence, will affect our own relationship. Whenever I ask him about what you said, he says that you didn't say anything. Never anything but "Hmmm" or "Umhmm." *What does that mean?* What is that supposed to be doing for Jake's problems—whatever you think they are? And when I ask him what *he* says to you, he only says, "Whatever comes to my mind." Period. What does *that* mean? Why can't I know anything? What is happening to him? We had enough trouble communicating before all this started. Jake only talks at the rare times when he's not feeling down, and for the last ten months (since he's been seeing you) he seems to be down all the time. What do *I* do now? Doesn't he need me to talk to anymore? I've tried several times during this past year to sit him down and have a rational conversation about why he is seeing you and why he's paying you so much for the use of your couch and the privilege of talking to you. He tells me it's *not my problem* and to mind my own business. Not my problem? Not my problem that a phantom may be pulling my husband away from me? Not my problem that a vampire may be sucking his blood dry? I'm *married* to this problem and I can't even find out what it is that has him so mesmerized.

Do you think it's quite fair to leave me out of all this? It seems like tremors are taking place in my hometown, and I am being kept from communicating with those I have lived with and fought with and loved with for all of my life. What will the tremors do to all of those people? Can they stand it? Will it change them? Will I no longer be one of them, not having shared that experience?

Of course, of course, of course I resort to words and metaphor. It is my medium, doctor. You know, in a real earthquake or similar disaster there is at least the Red Cross, which makes every attempt to reunite loved ones. Jake *needs* me. He can't keep up this silence. He loves me and he needs me; we know that we need each other. You must be influencing him to be so silent. Surely it is not your intention to make him withdraw even further into himself. I mean, even when I try to have a discussion with him, about sharing shopping or cooking for instance, I end up shouting my point of view while he puts on that Mr. Cool act and calls me a bitch. Do you know what I mean? Can you understand what it is like to try to get through to someone who thinks he's Clint Eastwood? Here, let me write out a short scenario for you. I'm sure he tells you about it quite differently.

ME: Jake, I really think we need to talk about food shopping and cooking meals.

JAKE: Ummm.

ME: [*Slight rise in volume*] Can you please put that book down for five minutes?

JAKE: [*Still looking down at the page*] I'm listening. You want to talk about shopping and cooking.

ME: [*Slight edge of anxiety in my voice now—like talking to my father when I was in high school and had to repeat my request to use the car*] Well—can't you stop for a moment?

JAKE: [*Irritated but controlled*] Talk, Jeanne, talk. You want to have a talk, so say something. I'm listening.

ME: [*Now I regress even further—like a child whining for candy as Daddy grows impatient*] Well, it's just that I have a lot to do now that I'm studying for my oral exams and I can't plan and shop and cook every night.

JAKE: [*Still looking down*] Then don't cook. Don't think you're doing me any favors with what *you* cook. Do what you want to do.

ME: [*Attempting a cheerful veneer*] But we still need to eat. I was thinking maybe we could share those jobs a little.

JAKE: [*Finally looking up, speaking sternly but still controlled*] Look, Jeanne, if you don't want to shop, don't shop. If you don't want to cook, don't cook. You're a big girl. You don't have to do anything you don't want to do.

ME: [*Softly now, afraid of an eruption*] OK. I won't cook. We can have TV dinners and sandwiches for awhile.

JAKE: [*Still a controlled, even tone—with a smirk as he looks back at his book*] You're a bitch, Jeanne. You're always competing, always trying to get me to do something else, never satisfied. You're just a bitch.

ME: [*Volume rising*] I'm not a bitch. I just have to speak up for my own rights. You just expect me to wait on you hand and foot like your mother used to wait on your father. He was working in the mines all day—you're sitting on your ass taking notes. I'm working as hard as you. Why should I have to do all the housework and cooking and shopping and balancing the checkbook and everything?

JAKE: [*Talking to book now*] Oh, here we go again. The poor bitch just has too much to do. The bitch is suffering so much.

ME: [*Damned tears beginning*] I'm *not* suffering, but I need some help. My schoolwork is as important to me as yours is to you. You think I should have to do all that just because I'm a woman.

JAKE: Poor bitch is crying again.

You see! He keeps all those feelings bottled up, only letting them out in sarcastic little bubbles that break in my face and sting my eyes. He'll end up like my father, with ulcers and heart trouble. And here I am trying to be logical and forthright, and I end up feeling like I've been naughty. Do you know, the really funny thing about all this is that an hour or two (or three or four) later when he climbs into bed he starts with the "Do you love me? Are you mad? Don't be mad with me" routine in the sweetest, most charmingly pleading voice possible. He comes back like a little child; he really does need me. Still, it all has to be on his terms. I must tiptoe around and be careful not to probe too deeply lest I "interfere with therapy." Apparently, things are so precarious that if I ask the wrong kind of questions I could set his progress back months or even years. I must not ask about the money; I must not ask about his progress; I must not ask what you, Dr. Frickman, have to say about his insatiable appetites; I must not ask what he thinks about the fairness of dropping his own dirty shirts at the laundry. (You may be surprised to learn that the little woman draws the line at ironing shirts!) What a neat little insulated box you allow him to build. Anything he'd rather not be hassled about is covered by that sacred declaration: "You're interfering with my therapy." Let us all keep silent before It.

Which takes me back to the original point of this letter. Why is he becoming even more silent? And why are you silent? Is your position so rigid or so mysterious and so holy that you can't even acknowledge my letter? You know, I told Jake about the letter I sent you; he *didn't even want to read it.* He gave me the that's-your-problem-Jeanne look and wouldn't even talk about it. You're both slamming doors in my face. Well, let me tell you, Dr. Frickman, now that I've begun writing I don't plan to stop. Whether you read these or not, whether you answer me or not, I'm not giving this up now. I've thought about writing for months and months. If I can't actually get either of you to listen to me, at least I can put it all down on paper. If I only understood what this silence meant. I just don't understand how all this is supposed to help.

Sincerely,
JEANNE DANIELS

November 10

DEAR DR. FRICKMAN,

I'm sitting at the kitchen table. You will forgive the narrow paper—it's my shopping-list paper and all that I have at the moment. (I thought of using toilet paper as a subliminal indication of my feelings about your treatment, but it's too difficult to write on.) I'm sitting here trying to understand, trying to maintain self-control. But I spent a good part of the afternoon making a coconut custard pie (*not* with packaged pudding but from scratch, with cornstarch and constant stirring, the whole number), and then preparing beef Bourguignon (I even stopped at the Italian market downtown for fresh mushrooms and tomatoes). It was all planned to be ready for Jake when he came in from school, and it was. I had started feeling badly about Hungry Man Salisbury Steak Dinner and Swanson's Turkey Dinner. No more! Do you know what he said after he came home and put his finger into the pie and took a few tastes of the beef Bourguignon? "Ummm, delicious. Did you really make this?" I accepted this offhand kind of praise and a kiss as my reward and started setting water glasses out on the table. Then:

"Don't put any out for me right now, Jeanne. I want to run over to the courts and see if I can pick up a quick game of tennis. I really need some exercise." He said this last as he sidled out of the room to change his clothes.

No more! No more, I say. He's been gone over half an hour, which means he must have found someone to play with. Here I sit. And I hate coconut and mushrooms.

Do you play tennis, Dr. Frickman? Perhaps that's a superfluous question. After all, you are a doctor, and I've noticed that tennis seems to be a requisite for the successful, admired physician. All kinds of bumbling idiots are out on the courts on the weekends with their green surgical-gown tops and little white shorts (secret identification), all attempting to develop an aggressive tennis style, a mean serve, and a superman backhand. One wonders what happens to them in the medical schools and in the hospitals to make them all so eager, so *driven* to dance around in their shorts whacking those little white balls. A safe place for competition? For releasing hostilities and tensions? For proving that they are sexually potent? I've read all those theories in one place or another, but none of them seems quite to explain the compulsive quality of the whole ritual. Don't get me wrong—I find an occasional game of tennis with a friend quite enjoyable, and I do all right at it. But there is one big difference between two men playing and two women playing together. Women talk to each other between sets or even while exchanging sides; tennis is a vehicle for social communication as well as physical exercise and friendly competition. But men just seem to be out there for the sake of whacking at each other's balls. They grunt and strain and look triumphant when they serve a ball that has such force it cannot be reasonably returned.

Well, that's neither here nor there. I really hadn't meant to write a treatise on tennis. But I *am* concerned about Jake and tennis. Maybe he does enjoy it. Maybe he has all the reasons listed above and several more for playing it. But this has become ridiculous. He wants to play or to serve balls or to hit against the wall every spare minute. He goes from hours of study to hours of tennis. He rushes out to the courts to get in a set or two before company arrives or before we go out for the evening. Dinner (even if all prepared) does not matter, chores do not matter, *I* do not matter. Mark my words:

if I ever have an affair (with one of any number of attractive possibilities), it will be because of this damnable tennis. We long ago
gave up playing together. It was too much a mirror of our everyday
lives, kind of like a speeded-up soap opera, with him criticizing me
for not holding the racquet properly, or yelling at me for not trying
harder to reach the ball, which he neatly sends first to one corner
of the court and then to another, and me complaining bitterly that
I am exhausted and that I need some encouragement rather than
abuse. At one time he even had me standing there for an hour at a
time simply returning his practice serves. Somehow, at some bright
moment, I realized how absolutely devastating such a passive role
was to my own development as a tennis player. As I say, we've given
up trying to play tennis together, although we'll take on an occasional mixed doubles match. (Naturally, I am always responsible if
we lose.)

I seem to keep wandering away from my main point in this
letter, which is, mainly, to tell you how fed up I am with this
apparent obsession with tennis. What does it *mean?* If I could only
understand, I might be able to deal with it better. Why must I be
kept in the dark?

Do you think this letter is about tennis, doctor?

(What do you think?)

I mean, am I making my point clearly?

(What point is that?)

Well, can you tell me if you agree with the theory that tennis
reflects one's sexual orientation and habits?

(What do you think?)

Well, would you agree that tennis and psychoanalysis have a lot
of parallels?

(What sort of parallels do you mean?)

Do you think answering a question with a question is a form
of hostility?

(Do you think so?)

Can you help me with this problem?

(The hour is up for today. We can go on with this tomorrow.)

As ever,
JEANNE DANIELS

November 16

DEAR DR. FRICKMAN,

After I wrote to you last week, I dreamed that both you and Jake broke your arms and neither one of you could play tennis any longer. Fortunately, I do not have to pay some silent listener thirty to sixty dollars an hour to hear myself figure that one out. Actually, I usually just tell my dreams to my friend Adam, a fellow graduate student down at school. He's in literature, too, but his mind is Jesuit-trained, and he has brilliantly logical, philosophical, intellectual arguments for everything. He has intense but gentle eyes, and he's a good listener—and one of the very few people I know who isn't always telling me his problems. That is, except for his psychosomatic (probably) stomach ailments. I didn't tell him yet about the dream I had just last night—more of a nightmare actually—about you. He'll be able to point out all the archetypal imagery and the Jungian associations. They may not be helpful for anything, but they are usually quite interesting.

Anyway, let me tell you about this dream. I'm excited about it because it was just so vivid. I was climbing a steep mountain—in Switzerland or somewhere like that—and whenever I looked up I could see beautiful snow-capped peaks and blue sky. But all of a sudden I came to a deep chasm with sheer, icy blue sides that seemed to stretch miles below the path. There was no way to turn back, and I was terribly afraid I wouldn't be able to get over that deep cavern. Then, there you were on the other side, holding out your hand— a Messiah figure, I guess!—saying, "You can do it, just try." But I just wasn't sure if it was all right to touch you. I was thinking, "No, this is my husband's analyst, I *can't* touch him." Then I fell. You know, I've heard people say you don't actually fall in dreams, but I did, a long, frightening fall. I woke up as I hit the bottom, my heart beating fast and my whole body trembling. The first thing I thought about when I woke up was whether this is how my father feels when his heart condition starts acting up.

So! Now I have a picture of what you look like, from the dream, I mean. I *have* to dream you up because my few careful, tentative attempts to get Jake to tell me about you—even just what you look like—made him recoil and withdraw as if I were a poisonous snake.

I'd say he's like a mother bear protecting her cub, but he's actually more like a man protecting the identity of his mistress, keeping always that aura of mystery, that hint of excitement. I want to *know* my competition at least, and that's why I'm dreaming about you. (Sometimes I think I'd rather he *did* have a mistress instead of you —at least the competition would be fair. This way it's like the crossbow pitted against the H-bomb.)

Having that dream and trying to imagine what you are like gave me the impulse today to dig out some old photographs of us, partly to show you what Jake looked like when I met him five years ago and when I married him three years ago, and partly to show you what *I* look like—not that you've shown any interest in me. Aren't you at least a little curious? I spent almost two hours choosing pictures, but since you don't seem to be taking the least initiative to answer my letters, I won't send you any pictures. However, let me tell you what the ones I picked out are like. First, imagine a slightly dark Instamatic print (taken by my good friend Genny) of a carefree-looking college-aged couple sitting on a bench under tall pine trees in the Catskill mountains (we were both working at a resort), arms thrown across each others' shoulders, self-conscious smiles for the camera—sort of the girl-next-door-fresh-face meets the strong, silent, hirsute cross between Paul Newman and Raskolnikov (we read as many Russian novels as we could get hold of that first summer, so I can't remember when I began to see him as a character out of Dostoevski).

And here's another Instamatic print, one of our very few wedding pictures (and again taken by Genny, who was my maid of honor). See how delighted I am to look at Jake—it's his boyish grin, his almost shy smile; even now I smile to think of it. Now look here at this one, taken just over a year or so ago—me still with my shoulder-length, strawlike hair, Jake with a definitely receding hairline. This one was taken on a camping vacation in Maine; we propped up my thirty-five millimeter camera on a boulder and set it on automatic to take our picture. You know what really interests me about this one? It's the reversal—in the issue of who is better looking I mean. It was about that time, getting close to age twenty-five, that I had honestly to capitulate, to admit, after years of teasing each other about this, that he was finally better looking than me. It's a sexist issue no doubt. His face does look older, but also more distinguished, more experienced and solid. Mine looks older too— see the white lines by my eyes from squinting into the sunlight? But how is it that I don't look *better* than my younger self as he does? For women, under twenty-five is considered most attractive (and a case could be made for even twenty being over the hill); but men, as long as they stay in reasonable shape, are considered as attractive (if not more so) after twenty-five. Note, please, that if I have gained some wrinkles, at least I have not gained pounds, as Jake has. Cut off my head and you still see the rah-rah, suburban, middle-class, long-legged cheerleader of yesteryear. Sigh.

But back to dreams for a moment; I've wanted to write to you for some time about all this dream business. I know how important dreams are to you and your comrades. There are lots of impressive precedents for taking dreams seriously, after all. Like Joseph's dream of seven fat cows and seven lean cows, which meant seven plentiful years followed by seven years of famine. And then there was the other Joseph's dream about going to Egypt and thereby escaping Herod's murdering soldiers. I'd be the last one to deny that dreams may have some significance; some dreams anyway. But don't you think this psychoanalytic business makes one pay an awful lot of attention to one's self? I mean, the minute Jake wakes up in the morning he's grabbing for paper and pen so he can write his dreams down—to have something to talk about with you, I suppose. I'll tell you, quite frankly, that I've read some of those dreams. They surely don't reassure me about your costly little conversations—or monologues or naps or whatever. Therapy, I suppose. (Is it more sophisticated to say "I'm in therapy" or "I'm in analysis" these days?) Anyway, why is my husband dreaming about other women? And why does he wake up each morning and grab a pencil instead of me? And then, why in the world does he leave these damnable scrawls right on the dresser top where I can't miss them when I'm either straightening up or putting his socks and underwear away? Surely it is no accident that he leaves those practically pornographic papers there? I feel like a third grader who can clearly see the words on the test paper of the best speller in the class. How can I *not* look when he doesn't even cover his paper with his hand? When I've asked him about these dreams, he has been, of course, very righteous and indignant that I should have read his notes and says that I am interfering with therapy.

To backtrack for a moment, what do you think my dream means? Maybe I don't trust you? Maybe I'm afraid you're holding out false hopes? Oh, damn, I know what you'll say. You'll see some deep sexual meaning in it, right? Some analytic double-talk about mountain-penises and cavern-vaginas. You'll take all the poetry out of it—like those psychoanalytic critic types who dissect in minute detail Alice's fall down the rabbit hole to Wonderland. I've read so much psychoanalytic criticism of that lovely little story that I can no longer consider it without thinking that when the White Rabbit mumbles about being "late for a very important date" (in the Disney version), he must mean that he is late for his analytic hour (with the Cheshire Cat, no doubt, who only grins and gives mysteriously contradictory answers to poor Alice's questions).

Listen, doctor, I hope you're planning a bit of a vacation for Christmas. I mean, we could sure use a little extra cash around here for holiday gifts and traveling home and all.

I am making every attempt to dream about fat cows.

Sincerely,
JEANNE DANIELS

December 1

DEAR DR. FRICKMAN,

You won't believe this. I don't think I do, especially since I'm still feeling so giddy and woozy and strange all over. What am I doing? (Yes! I keep asking my self that, What am I doing here? My self answers me, Dummy, this money will probably just go to that Dr. Frickman.) I'm making $125 for *one day's work.* (My God, who are you trying to impress, says my self—that must be peanuts to someone like him.) For what, you ask? For selling my body (and at this point I feel that my mind and soul have been called into the bargain). I'm sitting on the top floor of what I think is Presbyterian Hospital (I vaguely remember the name from a sign I saw when I got here at eight this morning with an empty stomach, ready to take two little pills). I'm sitting in a kind of waiting room of the Smith Kline & French drug research laboratory. I found this profitable bit of employment on the bulletin board down at the university several weeks ago, an innocent-looking little white three-by-five card which read: "Subjects needed for drug studies. Must be in good health. Four hours, $40." I jumped to call them. Jake and also Timothy and David and Michael from next door have since been used as subjects several times; usually they take a tranquilizer and then the nurses here monitor their pulses and the guys collect urine for four hours. They get $40 for it. The lab apparently doesn't use women often, but they needed one woman and one man subject for this particular test—diet pills (or so they told me). Could be LSD for all I know. Oh, not hallucinations or anything like that, but strange, definitely strange. The two of us who took these particular pills get a lot of money because in addition to taking our pulses and having us collect urine (in huge plastic bottles all clearly labeled with our names and set up here near us on a wall shelf!), they are also taking eight blood samples throughout the day. Notice how shaky my handwriting is, kind of scrambled? Well, that's exactly how I feel, like a mass of shaky, scrambled brains—which is a great deal better than the initial reaction I had of imagining I was dying or perhaps losing my mind. Now I'm almost enjoying this racing, dizzy feeling, even though the paraphernalia taped to my arm (for blood collection) makes it nearly impossible to pull down my jeans and pee into that bottle. Actually, I'm lucky I make it to the bathroom at all, considering the fact that I cannot yet (five hours after taking the pills) walk a straight line. Am I rambling? Am I making sense? Do you realize how crazy this is? When I carry my urine bottle out of the lavatory, its pale yellow level slightly higher, and set it on the shelf beside those of the other test subjects here (all male), I have this barely controllable urge to laugh hysterically. Everything, everything seems very, very funny. You. Even you, doc. Even you and your totally ridiculous treatment of my poor husband. Ha ha ha ha ha ha ha ha ha. Wow—I am flying so high, a mere kite in a beautiful breeze. But every so often I have this creepy feeling that I'm going to go low, low, low pretty soon . . . quite like I'm split in two.

Now let me try to pull my brains together. Why am I writing to you anyway? What a waste, right? Waste, waste, waste. Waste of paper. Waste of money. Waste of time. Wasteland inside your head, inside Jake's head, nothing but a vast wasteland, typical J. Alfred Prufrock types obsessing absurdly, "Shall I part my hair behind?"

David's here today, too, good old David, my dentist for the past two years. He works on my teeth once a week at the dental school clinic—like a long affair that never gets anywhere, if you know what I mean. (Yes, you *do* know what I mean.) I get low-cost dentistry and he gets his credits for gold foils and amalgams and crowns or whatever. We've established an interesting relationship—all that close physical contact *has* to make one feel a bit different about someone. There I am on my back, staring into his big blue gray eyes several hours every week (I need a lot of dental work). Anyway, today I've been telling David about you, and he's been telling me his rather ambivalent feelings about his girl friend. She's in Colorado or Arizona or someplace like that, and she might move here soon. He's very cynical but I just can't help laughing at his deadpan comments. In this high-flying state I'm in, it's all I can do to control an impulse to seduce him on the hospital cot I can see in an adjoining room. The way he touches me, both in the dental chair and out, makes me certain that he'd not offer any resistance. Jesus —I must be way out; I usually put only strangers in my erotic fantasies. He's only here at the lab for another hour (I'll be here for a total of eight), so I'll be losing him soon. Think I'll close now and talk to him some more. (I can hardly keep from constant talking under the influence of this pill.) I just wanted you to see what your expensive treatment of my husband is doing—to what heights it takes me—selling my body, my very blood and urine for $125 a day.

Yours,
JEANNE D.

December 10

DEAR DR. FRICKMAN,

It's 4:30 P.M., already getting quite dark, and it's freezing outside. That stretch of Indian summer weather must be gone for good now. A few years ago I might have felt sorry to see it go. But now all I can think is—no tennis today! I feel some need to apologize for that last letter. I was feeling so loose, so hysterical under those pills. I'm calmer now and you know, I've been thinking that maybe most of our problems—Jake's and mine, I mean—might be solved by this cold weather. Maybe tennis is all that's keeping us from a more communicative, satisfying relationship. We've been through a lot together—good times and bad—(all by ourselves) in the five years we've known each other, and we have all sorts of plans for years more together, including, by the way, babies of our own. (Neither of us can exactly say why, even when we've tried to be logical and rational about it, but we both feel that babies are somehow definitely in our future, and it might as well be sooner as later.) We've made it through lots of rough spots in the past. And maybe if he just stopped playing so much tennis he'd pay more attention to me again, and then maybe he wouldn't need you at all. Oh, I know that sounds very simplistic, but I'm just not convinced that he is really "sick" enough to need to see a psychiatrist five days a week. (Though I'll admit there are days I'd like to recommend some electric shock treatments to jolt him out of his selfishness.) He's just, well . . . he's just kind of young, not grown-up, I mean. I think a lot of that is caused by the prolonged adolescence of being a student. High school to college to medical school, always a structured environment, always working his tail off to please the higher-ups. I figure this motorcycle-tennis-no-domestic-responsibility-adolescent-selfishness stuff will have to end sooner or later. He'll have to grow up sometime, won't he? His father was a responsible man. Doesn't that count a lot?

Men are just such children sometimes. Even my own father, whom I now think of as an extremely responsible provider and mainstay of our family, even he had his less responsible, kind of escapist days when I was a little kid. I remember that my mother used to take my older brother and me to Sunday school—I must have been three or four and my brother five or six—while my father joined his pals at the firehouse on Sunday mornings. He was a volunteer fireman (talk about a childhood fantasy!) and they all got together on Sundays to polish up the big red fire engine. And on Friday nights he went bowling with his friends from work while my mother was left with us two little kids. She let us have cereal for supper on Friday nights; we thought it was such a treat. She must have been so happy not to have to cook dinner. What I'm getting at is this: She put up with all this kind of adolescent-out-with-the-boys behavior while always praising my father to us kids. We thought his backing the car out the driveway at breakneck speed when he heard the fire whistle was just the most courageous thing in the whole world, and we were convinced that he was also the world's best bowler. *He* grew up—not that he has ever given up his activities with the boys (golf later replaced bowling)—and he spent a lot of time with us all in later years. Maybe men are just like this; they retain that selfish childishness in them in a way that most women do not. Perhaps because women do most of the child rearing in our culture, men always see themselves as boys. Instead of going out with father to hunt for food or to plow or to drive away danger-ous beasts, as boys in a more primitive culture might, they watch their mothers do all the housework, shopping, clothing, and food preparation. They have little or no idea of what daddy might be doing all day. Women are called silly and irresponsible and passive and trivial. Hah! Where would men be without our patient, behind-the-scenes, responsible, active labors?

OK, I admit I was rash in saying tennis is Jake's main problem, but you might be at the opposite extreme if you've diagnosed Jake's problems as serious enough to need so much attention. I truly feel that I could tell you his problems in less than an hour (or even sum it all up in one phrase: the Pursuit of the Giant Phallus). And there are so many people around with much more serious problems.

I talked to two of them today. (I sometimes feel like Charlie Brown's Lucy with an invisible sign on my back that says "The Doctor Is In.") I was doing research in the library this morning and a friend, Evelyn, asked me to go out for coffee. She was polite enough to show concern about my upcoming oral exams, but the real reason she wanted to meet was that she was excited about a new plan she has for finding a husband. (Evelyn is twenty-eight, a medie-val history scholar, a virgin, hopelessly in love with a gay German professor. She lives at home with her sickly father. She's very de-pressed about most of these circumstances.) It's not that she has little to offer someone. Besides being quite bright, I suspect there is a rather flattering and feminine figure underneath all those high-necked, loose-fitting dresses. And if she didn't wear such practical shoes and pull her hair back in that librarian style . . .) We spent the rest of the morning (two hours) looking at the "personals" in the classified section of old copies of the *New York Review of Books.* We finally wrote the perfect ad calculated to get Evelyn a fine husband and eventual father for her two future children. Of course it's no use telling someone like that that marriage is no bed of roses or that the grass is always greener. She'll have to learn, like all of us.

Well, I gave up studying at the library after that. But home turned out to be no better. Timothy (another one of the guys in the next apartment) got home early because a clinic patient had canceled. He dropped in, ostensibly to borrow a meat mallet (he's something of a gourmet cook, and I sometimes eat dinner over there when Jake is on duty overnight in the emergency room or wherever), but apparently he really wanted to talk. Having trouble with his latest girl friend. (Last week he could only brag about how great she was because she loved anal intercourse—ass fucking, as he called it; today he could only talk about how "fucked-up" she is.) Timothy's father, who was a surgeon, died when Timothy was ten, so I guess his bed-hopping can be traced to that. What I find fascinating is listening to him describe his ideal woman one week, and the world's worst whore the next (same woman, of course). He's really very attractive—slim, tall, hairy, virile—and I keep thinking that if there *is* anything to this analysis business, he might be a good subject for you fellows.

Well, here I am, almost full circle it seems! I'm no longer questioning the validity of analysis, I'm drumming up business! But despite the meanderings of this letter, I want to reiterate that I do feel a lot of Jake's so-called problems are only a matter of growing up. And I hate to see him (and me) go through all this suffering when time may cure it just as fast. Of course, you're the doctor, and I cannot hope to equal your expertise. I'm just opting for a bit of common sense in this matter. Jake should be in any minute now, so I'll close.

Yours sincerely,
JEANNE DANIELS

DEAR DR. FRICKMAN,

Just a short note from my parents' home, where we're making our annual holiday visit before driving to Jake's mother's home in upstate Pennsylvania.

This is unbearable. I had hoped it might be different this year —because of analysis, I mean. If I haven't said it before let me say it now: If Jake ever was sick to begin with, he is not now getting well. If anything, he is worse.

As you must know, there is little love lost between Jake and my parents. My father was vehemently opposed to our marriage. I never quite understood why, although he had a variety of arguments, including: Wait until Jake is out of medical school and has started a practice; if you marry a Catholic you'll have to promise to bring your children up Catholic (woe to them!); you're always taking on problem people, and he's just another one; your backgrounds are too different; you're too young to make this decision. (Too bad my father thinks psychiatrists are crazy; think what an analyst he'd make.) Anyway, during the past three years of our marriage, things have naturally been tense, although polite, between my parents and us. A good deal of the responsibility for the uncomfortable nature of our relations belongs to my father and Jake. (It's true that my mother went along with my father three years ago. However, I'm convinced she did not especially agree with him, and was just being loyal. But she would do anything now to see things run smoothly.) I try not to take sides, though, and do all I can to break the almost visible ice between Dad and Jake when we all get together.

Getting stuck in slow-moving Christmas traffic and icy road conditions on the turnpike gave Jake and me an opportunity to talk before we got to my parents'. It was one of the best talks we've had in a long time. We reminisced about our Wednesday evening wedding. Just a few friends attended it, and we did not invite our parents. We all went out to dinner at some steak place afterwards and someone had bought a cake and stuck a dime-store bride and groom on the top. And I had to call my mother to tell her that we just got married. . . . She said she didn't know what this would do to my father. (I've often felt, over the years, that I caused his heart problems, ulcers, etc.) Anyway, Jake and I agreed, during this talk of ours on the turnpike, that we *had* been wrong. We should have included family and had a real celebration; we had cheated ourselves of something special, a *rite de passage* or whatever. That's the *first* time he's ever said anything like that. I felt like crying and I thought I glimpsed tears in his eyes. He seemed so open, so communicative, that I was really praising analysis (and you) silently in my head. And I was hoping that things might be different this year when we visited.

Well, your-patient-the-adolescent-egoist, their-son-in-law-the-medical-student ain't made no big hit again this joyful holiday season. For example, he insisted that he could only go to midnight mass at the Catholic church instead of to the candlelight service at the Protestant community church where my parents belong. Besides the point that the Catholics are practically the archenemy of Protestants like my parents in their town, I happen to know that Jake has recently dropped Christ for Freud. (Unfortunately, the only services being held that night were in honor of the former, not the latter, messiah.) He spent the better part of each day and evening with his books. He brought along his most impressive-sized textbooks on physiology and organic chemistry, and let himself be seen reading these studiously—and obnoxiously, I might add. And his expression when he opened his gift—a red and white knit ski hat with a tassel—was so tactless that it was really awfully hostile. "What? Me, Clint Eastwood, wear a red and white ski hat with a tassel?" he seemed to say.)

All this money being spent and he can't even be tolerant of my relatives. What is he always trying to prove? It's true my father likes to give advice, and it's also true that Jake cannot tolerate any "authority" . . . but surely at Christmas . . . and for just two days. I suppose I should be grateful that you decided to take this holiday yourself, so we don't have to pay for the days Jake misses, I mean. We're even taking a mini ski vacation with the money we're "saving." But for $150 a week, I had hoped for more from you. I'd like to see some statistics on the success of psychoanalysis. Bet that's all kept secret too, isn't it?

Happy Holidays, Dr. F.!
JEANNE DANIELS

December 30

DEAR DR. FRICKMAN,

Well, here we are in Vermont, with plenty of snow, excellent skiing conditions, comfortable accommodations at a kind of boarding house. I'm sitting alone in the lodge of the ski resort right now. It's almost four o'clock, and I'm exhausted. Jake, who only took one short break for lunch at 11:30 this morning, is obviously determined to be the last one up the chair lift before this place closes. That's what he's done for the past two days. We have to get here before the lifts are even operating, and he skis all day as if his life depended on it, or as if he must be sure to get his money's worth. To tell you the truth, doctor, and this is the reason I'm writing, I've been doing a bit of analyzing on my own (respectful of your absence here) while we've been on this mini-vacation and frankly, I'm worried about this behavior.

Why? Because I cannot believe it is really *fun* for him. I mean, it's just like his studying—start early, total immersion in activity, come up only for food, and finish late; all virtually without a smile. Oh sure, I guess he must enjoy it too, but not even a short break to rest his legs or let his gloves dry out by the fire (and for all I know, he must piss and even shit out there in the snow somewhere) or have a cup of hot chocolate with me, his wife, who is supposed to be a part of this vacation too? You know, now that I'm thinking about it, he makes other pleasures seem like work too. Eating for instance: He doesn't enjoy or savor as far as I can observe; he just keeps on eating, and at all hours too. If he falls asleep in front of the TV, and I wake him up to go to bed, he goes to the refrigerator first to eat a piece of pie or leftovers from dinner or whatever he can find, and he eats it standing up at the refrigerator, half-asleep. And he gets on these fads too, like buying that Sara Lee coconut cake every week for months, and before that it was those kosher pickles he couldn't do without. (I have some theories on those. In my literature courses I always like to search out the meanings of symbols, like Moby Dick the great white whale or Hemingway's glorified bullfights or Sterne's noses in *Tristram Shandy*. This search for the Giant Phallus is unmistakable and ubiquitous throughout the works of a great many highly touted male writers.) And while we're on this subject, I might point out that Jake's bedroom behavior has some similarities. I mean, we've been married for three years already. Could he *really* want to do it so often? Why do I so often get the feeling that I'm part of an attempt to prove something?

Look, I don't really like to get into this, but now that I've opened this Pandora's box, I don't want you to get the wrong idea, either. If Jake talks to you like he talks to me he must tell you I'm a castrating bitch, frigid, and hysterical, right? I want you to know that it wasn't always like this. Before we were married I was over-whelmed with passion. Just thinking about Jake made me feel ex-cited. But *his* neurotic, guilt-ridden Catholicism—much more than my WASPy, good-girl background—kept me a technical virgin until we were married, even though he had slept around plenty. And then we got married and the earth did not move, despite the virile Hemingwayesque character I had chosen for a husband. And he never can seem to forgive me for that. What happened? All that wonderful sexual excitement seemed to have been ruined by the priest's blessing (or could he have cursed this mixed marriage?). I mean, marriage sure brought me down from that unsoiled pedestal where I was treated with so much tenderness, care, romance, and just barely controlled passion. During the two years before our marriage we were at different schools and were often separated for weeks at a time. When we saved up enough money between us, I'd take the train to visit him on a weekend, and within five minutes of walking through the door of his apartment I'd have an orgasm —just from being held by him! You know what *I* think? I've been reading up a little (and sometimes a lot) in these popular sex manu-als, as well as in some technical psychology books in the library. I think I'm the victim of Jake's Madonna-Magdalen complex! *He* was only truly passionate while I remained an unsoiled virgin. Now, even though I've only slept with him, I'm a whore; he is utterly uninvolved with me even as he makes love to me as often as possible. Well, am I right? And if I am, can you *do* something about it?

On the other hand, I sometimes think it may be all my fault. Maybe I should have waited to get married, gotten a little experi-ence like the kids do these days without a second thought. They have no idea what it was like to be a teeny-bopper in the fifties, when going crazy over the gyrations of Elvis the Pelvis was the most rebellious and sexy thing we could think of. But it all seemed so fine with Jake before we were married; I had fantasies of being transported daily to Dionysian ecstasies—before he left the house each morning or when he came home for lunch or whenever we found ourselves alone in a seductive, scenic place like a deserted beach or far up the hiking trail in the forest. To tell you the truth, some of these fantasies, as far as the setting is concerned, even became reality. But, like I said, I've had a problem feeling that I really am part of it; he seems so out to prove something. Lately, I have found myself daydreaming about various strangers I have seen studying in the lounge at school or reading a newspaper in the subway or driving a truck up Broad Street. (Those truck drivers have a terrific vantage point for looking down at legs, if that's what they're into. I often see them, at the merest edges of my peripheral vision, looking at me, perhaps just waiting to be invited—or would that threaten them? What if I jumped out of my car at a red light and ran over to that sexy-looking guy in the laundry truck and suggested a quick roll amongst the bundles in the back of the truck? . . .)

Yet the very fact that Jake still wants to do it anywhere, anytime (almost) certainly makes me think it may indeed be my own problem. But I doubt it. Sometimes I think I need to prove to myself that I'm still OK that way, that I really do have that passionate, uninhibited self somewhere inside and that it is only his selfish, demanding manner that so often makes me uninterested. Smoking grass *does* help me get back to that self sometimes, but I never needed grass before to feel that high. Anyway, as I said, I have often thought of proving to myself that I'm really OK; there are certainly several bodies that might be willing to accommodate me, I should think. There's Adam, my logical, Jesuit-trained friend, but he's a romantic and a poet and you can never be sure about reactions with that type. I mean, suppose he decided he was in love or something like that? Anyway, he's a married man, and I have some sisterly feeling for his wife (even though I've never met her) just because she must have a lot to put up with too. Well, then there's David, our neighbor and my dentist; all that close physical contact—putting his fingers in my mouth and nonchalantly laying those instruments on my chest and all—has made me dizzy with desire at times. He's supposedly engaged to that woman in Colorado but fucking around anyway, so that wouldn't bother me. But he's so cynical and yet so mysteriously quiet, like a volcano that lets out ominous rumblings that only hint at what is going on inside. *That* I also don't need. Then there's good old Timothy, another of the dentists, the one who seems to get off on telling me about his exploits. Now *there's* a person with whom I would not have to fear involvement, and he *does* kind of turn me on. And I even like him. Of course he'd hate me after a few weeks. . . . Oh, fuck them all. I don't really want to do it anyway. I want to work things out with Jake, and have a family. Underneath that Clint Eastwood exterior he's a good man, and I think he'll be a good father, if he can just grow up a bit. Only recently has he begun to feel at all ready for a child; he *says* that's what he wants. Is it? Is my own wish for a child clouding my judgment about our situation, about our relationship, about Jake? I want him to be ready, to be grown-up enough to take on such a responsibility without panic. In practical terms, the time seems about right—me close to finishing my degree, Jake with only another year and a half of school. But how does Jake really feel? And what, *what* does he really want? Perhaps Shaw's Life Force is so strong in me that I see nothing but the possibility of procreation? *Is* Jake ready? Do you have anything to say about this? Say it now or forever hold your peace. (By now I expect you to hold your peace no matter what: You let us fuck up all we want and then call it "acting out." Isn't that the safest solution for *you?*)

Well, anyway. I just wanted you to know what "relaxation" means to my husband: skiing as if there were no snow tomorrow or no tomorrow at all. The pursuit of the pleasure principle is *work*. Now that I've stimulated myself by telling you my fantasies, I'm thinking about looking around this cozy lodge for some companionship, but I look like Raggedy Ann in this put-together, half-borrowed, no-match ski outfit. May as well get back to reading my Iris Murdoch novel (an old escape trick from childhood). Maybe I should pick up a copy of *The Scarlet Letter* or *Madame Bovary* or *The Story of O*.

As ever,
JEANNE DANIELS

January 10

Dear Dr. Frickman,

Happy New Year. That's a little late, I know. Actually, you see, after sending that last letter, I made a resolution not to write to you any longer. Here I am pouring out my inmost thoughts and feelings, and, for all I know, you may not even be reading these letters. Like analysis itself, it's just not fair. The way the situation is now, I might just as well be lying there on your couch (thank God I am not) telling you all of this, unable to see your face or your reactions. Maybe you just throw these letters away unopened. Maybe you just listen to him and think I'm a bitch, a nag, and/or an hysterical woman? Everyone listens more seriously to what men have to say, even when what they say is pure bullshit. I can remember as a child that my braggart, bullshitting, fabricating brother could always get my parents' attention so easily with one of his stories, even when I, a mere child and two years younger than he, could see right through his nonsense. So of course I really had to shine in order to get the same serious consideration—like women professionals or blacks or any minority group today. We are assigned "abnormal" or at least less than excellent characteristics before we even get a chance to show what we can do. Well, you can think what you want, both of you. If I *am* a bitch, a nag, or an hysterical woman, however, I can tell you that I have good reason.

Pick a day. *Any* day will do for an example. Take yesterday. I got home early from school (I'm teaching at the university this semester: freshman comp and an introductory fiction course) and sat down exhausted with a cup of Constant Comment tea to study for my oral exams. The king pulled up on his motorcycle at 6:30, hungry, asking about dinner. The little lady of the house suggested minute-steak sandwiches, since the hamburger for spaghetti sauce had not thawed, and anyway she was busy working. The king became incensed and informed the little lady that she could finish thawing the meat as she cooked it, at which time the little lady disappeared. The bitch entered and told the king about working hard all day and about concentrating on writing. He fumed and fussed about his own burdensome work, so the little lady came back long enough to make peace by cutting up green peppers and thawing the meat in the frying pan while reading about Mrs. Dalloway and her dinner party plans.

A short time later, after they had calmly eaten, the nag came storming in when the king wouldn't clean up the kitchen. Worst of all, however, was the appearance of the hysterical woman when the king announced his intention to go out to play handball at the Y. Her dramatic act was to no avail, of course, and after the king left, the bitch returned to scold the hysterical woman for once again being so vulnerable. (Damn woman just never learns.) The nag cleaned up the kitchen, making sure to pick up all the pieces of anger that were scattered about amongst the grease and rags and spaghetti, and she put them safely away in her deep pockets to save for another day. Even she knows that the pockets will fill and overflow at some point. But she knows that all of that anger might also feed the fires of her own desire to accomplish something outside this domestic situation. Angry woman? Sure, angry. Better angry, though, than condescended to, pacified by trivia, or placed on a damned plastic (or even chrome and glass) pedestal.

How *did* I get off into using third person here? I can hardly explain it myself—how I sometimes look at my own situation as if it belongs to someone else, someone whose actions and words I don't always understand. Do you know what I mean?

Anyway, back to first-person reality. Is Jake's behavior your "regression in the service of progression" that I've read about? Or is it just more male human nature? I mean, my father has always helped my mother out by cooking once in a while or vacuuming and even doing dishes after a holiday party, and not just when she's been sick or something like that. He's not afraid to do such a "feminine" chore. But of course he has limits, like all men. With some it's not putting away dishes or not polishing silver or not cleaning vomit —whatever they think is just too low to go. My brother, for instance, is now married and a father. He will not (1) clean a poopy diaper or (2) clean dog shit off the lawn before he mows it (he sends his wife out with a shovel).

Jake seems to think he'd be violating the laws of nature by cooking a meal or cleaning up afterwards or—and I've been thinking about mentioning this before—by scrubbing his own piss off the floor under the toilet and his own pubic hairs out of the tub drain.

If it's his mother he wants, he'd better go back home to live with her and leave me alone. What's the use? You're probably as chauvinistic as Jake is. May the Blessed Virgin and Martha Freud join in earnest prayer for you.

Very sincerely yours,
JEANNE DANIELS

January 21

DEAR DR. FRICKMAN,

La de da! He took out the garbage today on his own. And the *only* question he asked me about the process was where is the tie to tie up the bag. And after only one year of analysis. Let's see. At $30 a day, five days a week, about fifty weeks, that's just $7,500 to get the garbage out of the kitchen, down the stairs, and into the garbage pail. Figure the distance from the garbage can to the bin is, say fifty feet. That comes to about $150 a foot. Not bad! Let me congratulate you and the makers of Hefty Garbage Bags, who are always bringing us new ways to make life easier.

Did he tell you that I passed my Ph.D. orals? With no help from him, I might add. Did he tell you he kept bothering and pressuring me to make an apple pie the night before? To relax me, he said, so I would stop worrying about the exam. Keep those women in their places, eh, Dr. Frickman? Do you support this kind of behavior? I mean, barefoot and in the kitchen making pies? My examiners asked me about trains in Victorian literature. Trains. You know, like the train in Hardy's *Jude the Obscure* or in Dickens's *Hard Times.* My examiners were all men; obsessive-compulsive, neat, aging, gray-haired, and wise professors in ties and jackets all sitting there in front of me to see if I knew anything after all. I think trains are a very anal symbol, don't you? Chugging around the tracks, coming out of long dark tunnels, individual cars connected together. I've been reading all this literature for years and they ask me about trains. . . .

Well, anyway, I managed to pass. And you shall be the first to know my dissertation topic: a biographical and critical study of three women writers—Sylvia Plath, Virginia Woolf, and Zelda Fitzgerald. Are you at all a literary man, Dr. Frickman, or are you purely a man of science? My gynecologist can recite the prologue to Chaucer's *Canterbury Tales* in Old English. Very impressive—I told him while I was lying there, heels in stirrups, legs spread wide, with his fingers up inside me. People will do anything for attention, won't they? Anyway, in case you're not a Renaissance man like my versatile gynecologist, let me explain that the three women about whom I propose to write have one major characteristic in common: They all had mental problems. Two committed suicide and the other went mad. Virginia Woolf put rocks in her pockets and walked into the waves; Sylvia Plath put out glasses of milk for her two sleeping preschoolers and stuck her head in the oven; Zelda Fitzgerald suffered physical and psychological anguish in a mental institution before being burned to death in a fire. Do you like my topic? I expect it will be great fun all around.

Sincerely,
JEANNE DANIELS

January 26

DEAR DR. FRICKMAN,

I had another dream and it amused me, so I thought I'd pass it on to you. (Who else but an analyst could stand listening to someone's dreams?) This was a sex dream, just what you analysts must love to hear; evidence that the theories you're working with *must* be fact. Anyway, it was just a short dream. I was in bed with two men —Jake and . . . I'm not sure about the other one but I was really hot for him; perhaps it was Timothy. (He had just been over here again two days ago, telling me about this beautiful dental hygienist he was screwing. I can't figure out why I like someone who so obviously hates women.) Anyway, in the dream I really wanted to make it with this guy, whoever he was, but Jake wouldn't let me because, he said, what if I got pregnant? Nothing too hidden there, I guess, because I would like to get pregnant, I think. Just to think of having a child of my own—to hold and comfort; to teach to talk, to ride a bicycle, to enjoy music and dancing; to take to the library and come home to read together; to take on picnics and swim in the sea; to watch grow; to love. It makes me ache with anticipation. But what if I'm not really ready? What if *we* are not ready? Oh well, I'm not pregnant yet, and anyway, that was just a dream.

But speaking of dreams, I would like to get something straight in my mind. Do *you* figure out Jake's dreams or does Jake? He tells me so little about what goes on there, and he claims that it is *he* who figures out his own dreams—that, in fact, the person who has the dream is really the only one who can know what it means. Is that true? I suppose you think you've gotten to know him so well in the past year that you can interpret his dreams as well as he can. I'd sure hate to have someone see into my mind like that. And I'd sure hate to be your wife if you go around analyzing all the time. Being married to an analytic patient is bad enough.

I had a long talk with my friend Adam about this very subject, about this constant analyzing. Adam has been reading up on Freud too, though from a more philosophical standpoint, of course. Do you know the book on Freud by Ricoeur? Anyway, we started talking about why people would go into psychoanalysis, especially considering the great investment of time and money. Why not find an empathic friend just to talk things out with? I mean, is all that transference business really necessary? Suppose you somehow figure out that you don't trust anyone because your mother dropped you on your head when you were six months old. So *now* you know. Big deal. Or suppose you remember that your old uncle shamed you about picking your nose and you even managed to figure out that you associated nose picking with masturbation and so you had felt shame and guilt about that, and as a result repressed the desire to masturbate. So what? How can all that possibly help to make you a different person now and here in your present adult life? And even if it could, why not simply talk it all out with a good friend?

For example, after my long talk with Adam yesterday at school, Nancy came into my office and asked me to have lunch with her. Now she's in group therapy at the university medical center, but she likes to talk about the dynamics of the group as much as about her own problems, so I enjoy hearing about it. She's been divorced for not quite a year, has no kids, no binding ties, and is a promising, even brilliant scholar. (They toss that word around a lot in this department, but for Nancy, I tend to agree.) She's also beautiful—large, full breasts, full hips, and big, bright, blue eyes on a pixie face, not at all the stereotyped English scholar—and she happens to be a dynamic teacher as well. Nancy and I are also in a book group, a group of women that read novels and poetry by women, from Fanny Burney to Margaret Drabble. (The group, by the way, is another kind of enrichment in one's life; like a good friend, a group like that can help one think about one's self and support change, without necessitating being "in therapy.") Nancy has been seeing some fellow for several months now after an initial Irma La Douce imitation. He is a professor of mathematics, almost fifty (Nancy is twenty-six), a warm, witty, distinguished man who is seriously into culture—architecture, music, ballet—and travel. She'd like to hook up with him but she's afraid that would mean never having any family—any children, I mean. His life-style is firmly established: a beautiful little town house in the heart of the city, a loft full of books, a hospitable table with the best wines, a Steinway piano, and the sound of the Brandenburg Concertos filling the room from discreetly placed stereo speakers. She's right, of course. A baby (or, can you imagine, a two-year-old) does not belong in such an environment. Well, would analysis show that she was trying to "marry her father"? And even if it were true, *would it help* to know that? I could help her as much by listening empathetically and sympathetically as you or any analyst could when you listen and charge sacrificial sums of money for it.

I keep getting the feeling that I must be missing something. What in the world keeps Jake coming to you? And with all the worrying he does about money, too. You're not a friend. You don't even look at him while he talks. How do you make him so dependent on you? Why should he want to tell you everything? Or anything? He's been in analysis for a whole year now; that sounds like a long time to me. So I was quite disturbed to read yesterday that it is not uncommon for analysands to think of the first year of analysis as almost a waste of time, as only a period of adjusting, of getting ready for the real "work of analysis." Sigh. I'm telling you that Jake needs some friends to talk to. Or he could talk more to *me* for that matter. Why don't you get him to work at *that?*

Yours,
JEANNE DANIELS

February 1

DEAR DR. FRICKMAN,

As you probably know (or maybe it's not so probable, considering Jake's penchant for thinking about himself), I'm teaching full-time this semester, my first real professional position (although I've taught composition courses as a graduate assistant). I'm teaching two sections of basic composition and one introductory fiction course. Right now I'm riding quite high, feeling this to be a challenge, even a kind of adventure, as well as a performance—all of which I'm enjoying even more than I thought I would. Anyway, all that is a preface to what I want to talk with you about. (Did I say *talk?*)

I've been inspired to write to you this time because of an essay that I assigned my sixty freshmen composition students to read and then write about: "Psychology Constructs the Female, or The Fantasy Life of the Male Psychologist" by Naomi Weisstein. I came across this terrific article quite by accident in an anthology of prose readings. I was so amazed to read so much that I agree with, so much that I've felt to be true. Adam and I have had a wonderful time reading bits of it aloud to each other. For example: "Psychology has nothing to say about what women are really like, what they need and what they want, essentially because psychology does not know." Ms. Weisstein really puts down psychologists for looking for inner traits and generally ignoring social context, and also for having theories without evidence. What do you say about this study done in 1952—"an 'outcome of therapy' study of neurotics which showed that, of the patients who received psychoanalysis the improvement rate was 44 percent; of the patients who received psychotherapy the improvement rate was 64 percent; and of the patients who received no treatment at all the improvement rate was 72 percent." Well? The fact is . . . no, that's not fair, is it? *My conclusion* is that maybe Jake would do better on his own, without you, especially with the possible addition of a little common sense and maturity as he gets older. Think for a moment what it might mean to me, to us, for Jake *not* to see you five days a week. First, he would be home for breakfast—a very petty detail, granted, but after more than a year I'm tired of drinking coffee alone five mornings a week. Second, he wouldn't have to work all day Saturday to pay you, or if he did still go to work, he could spend his earnings on some relaxation or entertainment or a few basics around here. Third, I wouldn't have to have these part-time jobs and I would feel less resentful and our relationship would probably be much better. Fourth, Jake wouldn't be constantly looking inward, constantly interpreting and assessing every little incident, accident, and event according to the sacred Freudian code. And so on. I'm sure there would be other advantages to *not* continuing as well. But I have the feeling that you have him tied by some great umbilical cord, and that he could not cut through it even if he wanted to.

I'm telling you, Dr. Frickman, that what Jake needs is more *regular people,* friends to talk to, not just you, his analyst. Since he tells you everything, he apparently feels no need to talk to me or anyone else about his feelings or thoughts or anything, except on rare occasions. He has that direct line to you, that umbilicus, from which he thinks he receives all the nourishment he needs. Well, it's *not true.* I know this because I can see that he has this vicarious interest in my friends, in my relationships, and that he *needs* to know more about the outside world, so to speak, than he does. If I have had lunch with Nancy, or dinner with the fellows next door, or a meeting with my women's group, he wants to know "how is so-and-so and what is he or she doing about such-and-such?" I used to tell him a lot of what was said, but now I've become angry. He tells me hardly a thing about his outside life—not about friends or professors or nurses or patients, not even what he had for lunch—nothing. Why should I tell him a damn thing?

I've just paused in writing this, because of a sudden insight (you see, such things are possible even outside of the analytic situation). What I've been writing above is all leading up to something which

I, for some reason, want to tell you about. Kind of a confession, I guess, although there's really nothing to confess. Last Friday night Jake had to stay overnight at the hospital on emergency room duty, so I went alone to a party at Nancy's. Nancy, you may remember, is my bright, recently divorced friend. She had just a small get-together, an informal wine-and-cheese party for several of her friends and a few of Brook's friends (Brook is a mathematician she declares herself to be in love with). It was a strange group, to say the least, but I enjoyed myself immensely, especially after a glass or two of wine.

The group consisted of: a slightly built physicist of about thirty-five (also recently divorced) who wore horn-rimmed glasses and a gray sweater over an Oxford cloth shirt and who spoke very precisely and logically about any topic that came up; a single woman of about twenty-five who is a graduate student with Nancy and me, although neither of us knows her well—and we didn't get to know her too well that evening because she got quite drunk and loud and then fell asleep on the embarrassed physicist's lap; a married couple, both lawyers, who did a lot of talking about their ideal relationship, their mountain climbing in South America, their exhilarating sky-diving experiences, their fantastic skiing abilities, and the problems of their constipated dogs (of course, I couldn't help but be impressed); Brook, Nancy's very distinguished, intelligent, cultured friend who wore a beaded, Indian-looking smock and who was a warm and competent host, wise in the ways of making interesting conversation that included everyone, even in such a diverse group; and of course there was Nancy and myself; and one more—a thickly bearded young man with a gentle but intense expression, a poet (he has published two short volumes which apparently received some promising reviews) who is quite an accomplished jazz and classical pianist as well. Strange, that although I could describe to you in detail any other person in the room, right now I can hardly picture him—Randy is his name—except for his eyes, which seemed to say as much as he did, as much as his poetry does (for I have since bought both volumes), and as much as his piano playing did. I had arrived a little late at this peculiar gathering. Standing a bit awkwardly in the center of the small living room, I smiled and mumbled as Nancy introduced me to each person. When my eyes met Randy's, however, I felt a rush of excitement,

as if he were an old, well-loved friend, from another lifetime perhaps. I think he felt the same way, for throughout the evening,
through all the conversation, munching, smoking, drinking, and
music, we turned often to look into each other's eyes, without self-
consciousness, without questioning each other's meaning in the
least. Sounds like the someday-you-may-meet-a-stranger syndrome,
doesn't it? Well, I always was susceptible to such romantic notions,
but I feel convinced that this was somehow different, a deeper level
of communication.

Forgive me for going on so long, Dr. Frickman; I think I must
quite get the feeling that *I* am on your couch instead of Jake, which
is nonsense, of course. I guess I can only try to explain my wish to
tell you all this: I feel that my life is different, that I see Jake
differently, you differently, myself differently, and all from meeting
Randy and talking to him for just a few hours. About what? About
creativity, and mysticism, and man's inhumanity to man, about
relationships; nothing earthshaking. But even if I never see him
again (and it seems unlikely, since he does not live here in the city),
my life is changed. Can you understand that? I'm a little worried
because I have the feeling that this may make a difference in my life
with Jake. How could I have simply looked into someone's eyes and
listened to his music and felt an intimacy that I have been unable
to achieve with Jake in these years of trying? Why am I so absolutely
convinced it was not an illusion? Why, on the other hand, am I still
so drawn to Jake despite this lack of real communication between
us? I know, I know, you can't answer; but I must ask it: Why do I
love Jake so much—and I do—when I'm missing so much? Randy
hugged me as I was about to leave. A warm, unembarrassed hug
from a kindred spirit. . . . Time stopped for me in that moment; that
brief connection made me feel—how can I put it into words—as if
I were on the very edge of space, transformed into pure energy.

My God, how I've gone on and on and on. And I only feel a
bit more confused. I close now, hoping I won't be sorry for telling
you all this. These confessions have a way of making one feel silly
afterwards.

Sincerely,
JEANNE

DEAR DR. FRICKMAN,

Something is going on that I do not at all understand—and to tell you the truth, I am rather frightened. We've had arguments before, and we've had bitingly sarcastic verbal quarrels and wonderful tennis-court battles, and we've even had yelling, arm-waving fights, but I have never, in almost five years of knowing Jake, seen him violent. It seems to me that something is very wrong, that something must be bothering him very much. I'm scared. It's a little bit like the feeling I used to get when I had to ask my father a third time what he had said, that same anticipation of anger and displeasure, that feeling that I must tiptoe around and not do anything to displease him. Jake got so mad at me on Saturday—just a routine discussion-argument about sharing housekeeping responsibilities and handling our finances—that he kicked the oven door and threw a whole package of semifrozen lamb chops against the wall. I guess I shouldn't have mentioned your name; that seemed to have been the final straw. When he said he "couldn't deal with" the issues I brought up and that he just isn't "as emotionally invested" as I am in some things, I couldn't resist. All I said was something like, "You mean Dr. Frickman won't let you talk about our bathtub rings or my need for new underwear?" He blew up, he actually blew up, and that's when he kicked the oven and threw the chops. When I pointed out that I had no emotional investment in the damn lamb chops, I really thought for a moment that he might punch me. I knew I was pushing it, but I had hoped to make him laugh. He was in no laughing mood. He seems to have surprised himself with the depth of his anger. I think he even realized he couldn't really have been that angry with *me*. So what's happening? Did I inadvertantly step into the middle of some kind of transference crisis? He loves you? He hates you? You love him? You hate him?

What is wrong? WHAT IS WRONG? I've been secretly digging into my books on psychoanalysis again, hoping to find some description of this as a reaction to something, or as a "normal," transient phase of analysis. Is this progress, some of those stored-up feelings coming out at last? Is this Clint Eastwood of the calm exterior finally shooting his guns off in an impressive display of aggression? Or is this a regression, back to two-year-old tantrums at having his desires thwarted? *I don't know. I don't understand.* Why am I left alone in this process to struggle with all of this? What if you can't help him? What if all this doesn't come out right? Are you sure he can take this, whatever it is that's causing these feelings of violence, I mean? Are you sure *I* can take it? Are you sure our marriage can take it?

I talked to Adam today. Poor Adam has to be *my* psychiatrist every once in a while, probably too often. He doesn't usually offer any direct advice or anything like that. It's just that having a calm talk over a cup of coffee, a talk about our teaching or about poetry or our dissertations or our professors and fellow students, makes me feel that the world is OK again, that I'm a person in my own right, a person to be listened to and taken seriously. In fact I feel like quite a different person. I don't feel obliged to say the right things, to do the expected. Adam is a good listener, and more than that too, a good talker. I mean, he contributes a lot to a conversation, whether we're talking intellectually or emotionally. (Why do I feel that my discussions with Jake are so one-sided? I could write him letters like I do to you. And I wouldn't be sure he'd read them either.) But even *I* realize that it's not fair to talk to Adam about my problems with Jake so often. I need *you* to *do something.* I need to understand what is happening. I feel like I'm swimming around in icy waters under thick layers of dark ice, frantically searching for an air hole to come up in. There is very little light filtering through, and the cold water is beginning to make me numb, unable to keep searching for that place where I can come up to breathe. I had this frightening dream last night in which I saw myself standing very still with a big frozen smile, inside a mirror, trapped, passive, lost. I (my other self, outside the mirror) was crying, hitting the silvered glass trying to break it open so my trapped half could get out. Ah! I can hardly bear to think of that again.

By the way, Jake has reiterated to me that he does not care if I write to you and has no interest in reading what I write. I complain enough out loud, he says. And rest assured that he has passed on to me your explanation of your policy not to have any contact with anyone other than your patient unless you all decide it would be beneficial to get together for a session or two. So look, I know you can't—or at least won't—answer this letter. I know you won't talk to me if I call you on the phone. But won't you please do something with Jake—stop whatever it is you've done to him? I don't want you changing him. I love him and I want him the way he was.

I mean it.
JEANNE

February 10

DEAR DR. FRICKMAN,

Let me try to express this as neutrally and as impersonally as is possible in this triangular situation. Pretend, for a moment, that I haven't written a word to you for these several months. Let me try to be completely objective. I'm writing to inform you that your expensive treatment does not seem to be helping my husband a bit. He was self-centered, indeed selfish, to begin with. But during these thirteen months of seeing you five mornings a week he has become unbelievably absorbed in himself. Do you really think it is good for a person like that to start examining his life in detail? For example, we went to visit his mother this weekend. (I guess he told you that already, but I think you ought to hear more of this stuff from another point of view.) Now, his mother is not a selfish person. She has always worked hard and even helped put Jake through college, and she always makes him his favorite dessert, coconut custard pie, when we go to visit her, and she won't let him help with the dishes, and she makes sure her only son has enough pillows under his head when he stretches out on the couch to watch TV. Now, how do you think he repays her for all of this sacrificing and attention? Me. He gives her *me* for the weekend. He goes off to see his old small-town cronies at the poolroom, and I get stuck with an unending quiz.

"So how is Jake doing at medical school?"

"He looks thinner."

"Are you feeding him enough?"

If she asks *him* anything, he answers with smart-alecky cracks or monosyllables.

"I'm trying for that 'lean and hungry' look, ma. Think it will help me be smart?" No respect. No sensitivity.

Needless to say, his mother never read *Julius Caesar* and takes all his comments seriously. I can see she looks worried, and of course she asks me about it when he's gone. I wouldn't mind so much if he wasn't at least fifteen pounds overweight.

When he does come home, he quizzes *her* about his childhood. And it's cruel—really mean—this obsession with knowing all the details of his early life and making his mother feel guilty. "Didn't you and daddy sleep in different rooms when Cynthia and I were small? Why? How come I spent so many nights over at Nana and Poppy's? Did I sleep in their bed? How old was I when my cousin Paul came to live there? Where was his mother? Did you let me pee out the second-story window once when I was about three?"

Did you tell him to ask her all this?

These are all obviously family secrets, and he just asks them, demanding answers from his poor mother right in front of me or his sister or whoever happens to be there. (I remember reading someplace that a man will treat his wife as he treats his mother. Sure enough he bullies her like he does me. But I should learn from her. She remains stubbornly silent and holds her own ground if she doesn't want to answer him.) The point I'm trying to make is: Don't you have any rules about these things? Why is he trying to blame his mother for his so-called problems? Alas, I know. The mothers get all the blame. I saw my own mother constantly giving in to the lordly authority of my father. Sure, he's a smart, good, strong, even kind man, and even though she's just as smart and good and strong and kind, she's always had to go along with him. She could have done great things, perhaps. What did she get out of being submissive and sacrificing all her time to us kids and my father? Overwhelming praise? Riches? Fame? No, the mothers are responsible for all the bad things and get no credit for the good things. Unless they are totally submissive and subservient they are bitches or castraters and overprotective hysterics or domineering neurotics. And all that without the power of the mighty phallus. My, my.

What is your mother like, doctor? Do you have her on a pedestal, as Freud had his mother? Is she oh-so-proud of you, her son the doctor? Or do you blame her—for casting you aside perhaps at the birth of a sibling, or what's more to the point, for casting you aside when daddy came home? Oh! Too personal now, doctor? Excuse me, so sorry. But you see how all these personal, penetrating questions might upset Jake's poor mother, don't you? *She's* not in analysis, after all.

As ever,
JEANNE DANIELS

February 15

DEAR DR. FRICKMAN,

Happy Valentine's Day a day late, Dr. Frickman. Pooh, such hypocritical rubbish: valentine hearts, candy and laces; keep those women in their places. It almost makes me want to tear off my clothes, grow wings like those cherubs on all the flowery cards, and run around shooting arrows into a lot of male hearts. Especially yours and Jake's. Hmm, what a pleasant little fantasy . . . and just look how it supports your intellectualized theories about sex and aggression. Actually, Jake has become, under your tutelage, quite an expert on these topics. This is a direct quote from him regarding the basic drives of sex and aggression: "What anyone always wants is to get laid, and to kill everyone." Nice succinct phrasing, very neat. You, doctor, are accomplishing wonders. You know, I wouldn't have minded it so much if Jake had said it just to me. But your idiotic patient came out with that gem last weekend as we were having dinner with my friend Evelyn and a fellow who had answered her searching-for-a-husband ad in the *New York Review of Books*. (She didn't want to be alone with him on the first date. Last month some engineering type had apparently tried to rape her after the symphony, or at least so she told me.) This fellow, Evelyn's date, was extremely nervous right from the start: hands shaking, stumbling over his words. Only when I got him talking about his area of expertise (some kind of involved experiments with drosophila) did he calm down a bit. Jake made his comic statement in some conversation that involved Evelyn's cat, who was apparently in heat and was therefore howling to get outside. Evelyn's date, Nelson was his name, was trying to make some point about the usefulness of animal studies, especially those involving primates, for understanding human behavior. That's when Jake simplified it for all of us by telling us what it is we all really want—to get laid and to kill. Poor Evelyn turned beet red and Nelson picked up his wine glass and promptly dropped it. Truly embarrassing. I don't think Jake even realized the effect his words had.

But let's get back to Valentine's Day for a moment. Tell me, doctor (rhetorical phrasing, of course), did you get a card for your wife? A box of candy, flowers? Since I have fussed about this annual holiday during the past three years, Jake did truly make an effort to acknowledge it this time. It was certainly a big improvement over last year, when I got just a card from him with a picture of two hillbilly folk on the front—you know, missing teeth, knobby knees, carrying a jug of whisky—with the message reading something like, "Be my moonshine 'cause I'm sure moony about you." Or maybe it was cleverer. I've really tried hard to forget about it. Well, yesterday Jake came home from school with a heart-shaped box of chocolates and a card. When I opened the card I could have fainted with surprise. It was one of those romantic photograph cards—a hazy silhouetted picture of a couple holding hands, walking along the beach at twilight. Inside, however, under the romantic little message, he had written his own message: "I love you very much. Don't be mad that I'm going to play tennis as soon as I come home. Love, Jake." He was already upstairs changing by the time I read that.

I gave *him* two cards, by the way; did he tell you? Perhaps an indication of my ambivalence or of my schizoid character or of Gemini, my astrological sign? Make of it what you will. One card was, like his, a romantic kind of valentine. The other was a card with a Rorschach-type inkblot on the front and inside a message that read, "I don't know what you want." And *that* is the truth. What in the world does he want? To play tennis every day, to have no real relationship with me—or with anyone else except you—and to make a lot of money and never spend it? Is that what he wants? Well?

Sincerely,
JEANNE

February 23

DEAR DR. FRICKMAN,

Money, money, money, money. He talks about it all the time and is always afraid we won't have enough (for what, I ask him), even when we have managed to put some small amount into savings. It is true that I may be too much on the other end of the spectrum —if we have money I tend to spend it without much thought—but his inability to spend and his desire to save seem beyond normal limits of economy. I'm sure that thrift is a fine old quality, but El Cheapo is a lot more than thrifty. How in the world do you get him to pay you so much money every week? I can't even buy flowered toilet paper without having him complain that it *must* have been more expensive.

Sometimes I wonder if having had to pay you so much has made him this way, but in thinking back, I guess he's always had this tendency. The Christmas before last, for example, we had talked about buying a stereo with the money my parents had promised as a gift plus some of our own savings, as a treat to ourselves. We even became quite enthusiastic talking about what records we'd like to own—the Beatles (for old times' sake), Gregorian chants (for studying, thinking, and relaxing with tea), Cat Stevens (for brightening up dull November or February days) and Pachelbel's Canon and the Brandenberg Concertos (for a sense of grace and permanence and beauty). I started reading up on stereo components in *Consumer Reports* and priced them at several stores. When I had finished my research, I took him to the stereo dealer and we listened and compared and discussed—and went home empty-handed. When we got home, however, he told me I could go back and purchase the one we had picked out. He *couldn't stand* to be there writing out that check!

His mother told me that when he was a child, he carefully saved any money that came his way. When he wanted something, he wheedled money out of his mother or father or sister or grandparents. Maybe it's a male-equals-money or money-equals-male problem. Is it that his self-esteem depends on having money in the bank? (In that case, all he needs to raise his self-esteem is to quit analysis. . . .) Seems to me I've read somewhere that saving money is somehow connected with saving feces—with being constipated, then? Damned if I can figure out what that has to do with anything. Unless psychoanalysis is one big enema . . . getting it all out. (I guess I must be entitled to some free free-association sometimes.) This constant worrying and talking about money really makes me quite weary. And the more I think about it the angrier I get! I mean, look, he's paying you a hundred and fifty dollars a week, right? A hundred and fifty dollars spent on himself, his own self-improvement if you want to call it that. Well, why am I not entitled to a hundred and fifty a week to spend on myself, on anything I'd like? I do most of the chores and bring in more than half of our income besides. Let me choose something comparable; let's say I wanted to spend a hundred and fifty dollars on this fantastic Gypsy palm reader on lower Broad Street. What would happen? We'd have to sing for our supper and our rent money, and we'd also build up quite a debt. This analysis makes us downright poor! Even paying you a "low" fee is an extravagance beyond words. I don't ask for new furniture (our Goodwill Antique has character) or designer clothes (my jeans and a new turtleneck now and then are right at home on campus) or luxury cruises (I like camping as long as there are toilets and showers). I just don't want to feel guilty for buying some new underwear or a new pair of shoes or a cherry cheesecake from Pierson's Deli or even hoagies from Lee's on a Friday night. Is that too much to ask? Don't I deserve that much?

So what is it, doctor? Why does it mean so much? Why is he living as if we were in a depression? He plans on becoming a neurosurgeon. I believe they make a good amount of money (and have an ego problem to match, I understand), so what will he *do* with that money?

Well, I just wanted to tell you that I'm going out, as soon as I finish this letter, to buy a new winter jacket and gloves. And I'm not going to feel guilty. I'll only be spending about as much as he pays you for two analytic hours, and anyway, February is a short month so he won't have to pay you so much. I bet your wife is walking around in a cashmere coat that costs the same as fifteen analytic sessions. And she doesn't even have to listen to Jake!

Sincerely,
JEANNE DANIELS

Part Two

February 27

Dear Dr. Frickman,

Did he tell you? He *must* have! We did it! We did it at last! Four months of charting my temperature, four months of cutting down on sex (in order to have more sperm when it really counts), four months of propping my thighs up on pillows to make sure. Last week Jake took a urine specimen to school; it was negative. But yesterday he took in another one—and we did it! I'm pregnant. I threw out all my packets of birth-control pills. We've begun a new phase of adult life. Maybe having a bit of difficulty getting pregnant was a good thing for us; I mean, no presto-magic-you're-pregnant trip to deal with. And oh, how cherished this child will be. (Don't worry, not too cherished, doctor.) Of course our lives won't be changed much for awhile. I'm continuing with my teaching at the university, and I plan to spend all my extra time working on my dissertation. I hope to finish it before the baby comes (late October is the target).

You know, I just thought of something: Maybe you've been following this story, so to speak, for months. You've known about that damned thermometer, about less frequent sex (which, by the way, was fine with me), about which days I ovulated, and about our false hopes when my period was a few days late a couple times. Maybe Jake talks about all this stuff in his analytic hour. Hmmm.

I have another reason for writing. Ecstatic as I am about all this, I'm somewhat afraid of how it will affect Jake. Is he ready to take on a new, huge responsibility like this? Didn't I read somewhere that one is not supposed to make any big decisions while in analysis, or something like that? I've wanted a child for a long time—with mixed feelings because of graduate school and our relationship—but Jake always wanted to put it off. What made him decide that *now* is the time? True, he'll have only one more year of medical school, and I have "only" my dissertation left to do, but could such timing be the only reason he became so interested in having a child now? You must know the answer to this much better than I do. Yet *I'm* the one who is pregnant.

Do you have any children? Are we in competition with you? Or is it the old story of being in competition with his own father? I *have* thought that lately I've observed him behaving a bit more like his father (whom I knew only for a brief time two years before he died). Or is he trying to outdo his sister, Cynthia, who is expecting next month? Does that have anything to do with it? Perhaps it is best not to ask such questions (I certainly can't ask Jake these questions), but they are there on my mind, not to be denied. And so I must ask you—silent, stone-wall, imagined listener.

(So often I ask myself, who are you, Dr. Frickman? Let's see, it's John Frickman, isn't it? Who are you, John? Who are you to know so much not only about my husband, but also, by reason of propinquity, about *me* as well?)

Ah!—today I'll not think about any of this nonsense. I have a baby growing inside me! We will have a baby to cuddle and love and watch grow. It's difficult to believe that anyone else has ever experienced these same sensations of excitement and joy—isn't that strange?

Sincerely,
JEANNE DANIELS

March 15

DEAR DR. FRICKMAN,

As you must have noticed, I haven't written for a couple of weeks. Not to worry, though; I've been very busy pursuing my own madness—my dissertation, that is. I think I have some interesting points to make concerning the madness of the three women, especially concerning their relationships with their respective fathers. (Can you see it in print? "Fathers and Literary Daughters") Next, I'd like to compare their fathers with their chosen spouses and then consider the male-female relationships that these particular daughters write about.

Which brings me to my reason for this epistle. Good Lord, how *do* people choose their spouses? More specifically, how did Jake and I choose each other—or didn't we? You know, when I was an adolescent, or perhaps a bit younger, I was a faithful reader of the horoscopes in the daily paper ("Attend to an important business matter this A.M. and relax into a romantic interlude in the evening.") and in the teen fashion magazines ("This month your sign moves under the influence of the house of Jupiter. Expect some disappointing news early in the month, but romance and passion will have a place in your social life during the latter part of the month."). Even in my religious-fanatic phase (my adolescent rebellion took this form), I still secretly invoked the power of those promising horoscopes. I blindly hoped for what was supposedly written in the stars for me. I don't think I ever actually *believed* that my fate lay in the stars (I was, after all, an all-powerful, all-knowing, anxious adolescent), but I certainly must have received comfort from those optimistic words (always tinged with a bit of pessimism to add to their realism).

Now I can look with scorn at astrological predictions. For of course, our fates are not written in the stars. The heavens cannot predict or identify Prince Charming or even his white horse. I need no longer try to remember what all those articles in the magazines told me about the viability of a marital relationship between a Gemini and a Sagittarian. Who needs the stars any longer? The astrology charts have been replaced by a much greater system— *psychoanalysis.* Fate is not in the stars; rather it is to be found in the first three years of one's life. And one need not worry over the choice of one's mate, for that too is all determined in the circumstances of one's own past.

It is quite easy, really. I've learned all about it, you see. One's choice is unconscious, another neurosis to complement one's own neurosis. One marries a substitute for one's mother or father or sister or brother. The only problem, then, is figuring out which of these one is fated to marry, or, as in my own case, which ones Jake and I have married. This can all be revealed in the scientific practice of psychoanalysis. A bit more expensive than the horoscopes in the newspapers and magazines, this process, but that's not what I really object to. I just want to know *which one am I?* It never took too much insight to perceive that he saw me as a kind of mother figure, pushing my tolerance to the limit, expecting always to be taken care of, to be accepted and loved no matter what. But he has lately been talking (never with any real coherence, only in hints here and there) about how much I am like his *father.* And to top all that off, I seem to many people to *look* like his sister, who is also twenty-five and is in the same family position as me—second child with an older brother.

I don't want to be his mother or his father or his sister; I want to be *me,* Jeanne. Jake is so wrapped up in himself because of psychoanalysis that I'm not sure that he *does* any longer see me as *me.* A simple argument about which movie to see can turn into his condemnation of me as "competitive." I know then that I'm his sister Cynthia to him.

Look, doctor, you've gotten us into this mess, this unreal kind of living and reacting and interacting, and, as I see it, right now you're the only one who can get us out. I have to trust in you as blindly as I trusted in those horoscopes; I have to hope that you can read the origin of our fates, that you can help order the present, and that you have some insight into future alternatives. Your "psychoanalese," your scientific phrases and terms, mean little more to me than all that astrological jargon. To me, the Age of Aquarius promises as much as the Age of Freud. I love this man, my Jake, doctor; I love the person that I feel deep within him—through his silences, through his (sometimes) coldness, through his joys, through his disappointments and griefs. Why must I be left out now that he has you? Where is your humanistic understanding to allow a spouse to be placed in this position—for *years?*

Very truly yours,
JEANNE

Dear Dr. Frickman,

You know, it should certainly have hit me before this, and I guess I *did* think a bit about it in some rather abstract way, that being pregnant with Jake's child makes us doubly (or more than doubly) committed to this marriage. I mean, whatever happens now, for better or for worse *("for richer or poorer")* this other being —our child—will be affected as well. Such a realization, it seems to me, suggests at least two possibilities concerning Jake's behavior. He may quite suddenly realize that he is at last an adult, a grown-up who must take charge when he is needed by those dependent on him. Or, at the opposite end of the spectrum, he may feel the walls of this nonstop elevator slowly closing in on him, bringing to an end these casual, relatively carefree days—and he's going to want out! Right now I'm not able to see which way he is going because he "can't deal with" talking about it. Why the hell not? I'm the one who's pregnant and *he* can't deal with *talking* about it. Don't tell me that even becoming a father is going to be a completely narcissistic experience for him (please don't tell me that). I do have a part in this, you know. And you, doctor, you too, it seems, have a part in this, for you will be able to ascertain from your position at the helm (bow end of the couch) which way he is turning, and perhaps do a bit of steering as well.

It's odd how seemingly unrelated facts or events sometimes almost jump together to make one realize something important. I mean, the reason this whole commitment question hit me is because of several things that have been going on in my life recently.

Jake and I went to see Ibsen's *A Doll's House* this past weekend with our friends Sydney and Mandy (he's a lawyer; she teaches English at a private school). I've read the play before and knew what to expect; that's why I was surprised to find myself so angry at the lack of respect shown Nora, especially by her husband, and so moved by that ending in which Nora, her husband's "little squirrel" and "little sparrow," so astonishingly resolves to leave not only her husband but her children, too. How this must have affected an audience in 1879!

Quite by coincidence, I've been reading a novel out of the same period, Kate Chopin's *The Awakening*, a book that has become quite popular in the women's movement. I had read it for my women's book group two weeks ago. In *The Awakening*, the heroine, Edna, after a stormy period of passion for another man, also resolves to leave husband and children; she commits suicide by swimming out to sea and allowing the sensual waves to envelop her naked form.

Two good dramatic stories, but stories that can only make me ask a lot of questions, especially when I try to place myself in either Nora's or Edna's, or even either of the husband's, shoes. I mean, *where* does Nora go? How will she live? What will become of her children? How will she feel for having left them? And Edna—*must* she have committed suicide? Could she not go and find some happiness with her lover? Was her suicide really better for her children than a scandal? All these are questions that anyone watching the play or reading the book are bound to ask if they are moved at all.

But now to another, more relevant kind of question. Consider: What, just what if either Torvald (Nora's chauvinistic, condescending husband) or Mr. Pontellier (Edna's husband) *had been in analysis at the time?* Can you imagine how that would have changed things? Just think of Nora, timid as she was, feeling angry at Torvald for spending all that money on analysis, and think of her worrying about what he was going through at the time, wondering if he really would change, hoping he would finally stop calling her "little sparrow." Think how paralyzed she must have felt. And Edna. What if her cigar-smoking, conscious-of-social-appearances husband should have been seeing an analyst four or five mornings a week? Would she have said to herself, "Well, he's a silent fellow and a cold fish, but he's trying to change, so I must sit by patiently and hope for a change"? Would she have refused to allow herself any passion outside of marriage? Would she have stood on the beach and thought, "Suicide would be sweeter to me than this life, but oh, oh, what of Leonce who is trying so hard in his analysis"? What do you think?

And now, back to our very own scenario. Do you realize, doctor, what an influential factor you are in our lives? Somehow, you are an inherent part of all our decisions, a kind of invisible judge in all our arguments, a seemingly benign onlooker at the zoo who watches the monkeys with amusement from his superior position outside the cage. But you are far from a benign observer; you are a participant merely because you are *there* five mornings a week, sometimes a father confessor, sometimes a superego, sometimes an inescapable brick wall. Sometimes I even think you're there in bed with us, and I'd like to kick you out—but I'm afraid of what Jake would do.

Alas! I begin to scare myself with my own fantasies. Let's see, I began with this question of commitment to each other and the question of Jake's either taking more responsibility or retreating further from it. What will happen now, doctor? That is what all this comes down to. You really had better help him steer toward a course of responsibility.

I have also just been reading Ernest Jones's biography of Sigmund Freud and learning about Mrs. Freud, who gave birth to the great man's six children. While she sat at home, her husband and her sister went off traveling to Italy and wherever. Mr. Jones would have us believe it was all very much on the up and up. But I wonder, I just wonder how Mrs. Freud thought of it, sitting there trapped at home.

If you do have any power at all—and I believe you do—please make him grow up. I will not be trapped. I will not be bullied or condescended to by either of you. I'm not threatening to follow Edna's example. But Nora's example, I sometimes think, is not so farfetched.

Sincerely,
JEANNE DANIELS

March 24

DEAR DR. FRICKMAN,

I really must apologize for my last letter. I think it's being pregnant that just makes me feel so . . . so volatile, so emotional. I really do not mean to be angry with you, or with Jake either. Sometimes I guess I just let my imagination run away a bit too far. Maybe Jake is right; maybe I live too much of my life in books. Although sometimes I feel quite the opposite. There are so many people around me who seem to need to make some kind of connection that I don't have nearly enough time for my books—and especially for my dissertation. Why, just in the past few days I bet I've spent five or six hours listening to various friends sort out their problems. Nancy, for example, has finally decided to move in with Brook, and we had a long talk about how much a woman "needs" to have children to fulfill herself and how much a man "needs" to have a woman bear him children to fulfill *himself*. Of course we were both talking blindly. I have no real reasons, no good explanation of why I'm carrying this child (other than the usual biological facts of the case), and Nancy has not yet even seriously considered having a child. Anyway, Nancy and I had a long discussion about whether it is harder to *combine* children and a professional career or to work wholeheartedly to have a career *instead* of children. Between the two of us, I guess we'll find out sooner or later. Nancy is such a nurturing person that it is difficult for me to see her opting for childlessness. But we'll see.

I also had a very long talk with Evelyn, whose mind seems to run in only two channels: medieval history, in which she's been doing a lot of research, specifically on the topic of alchemy; or on getting a husband and having children. It is so obvious that she is still so in love with that gay German professor (old enough to be her father, anyway), but she seems to be opting for the Life Force, for bearing children. The few guys we've sifted out of the returns from her ads in the paper have been, more or less, losers. There was one rather rich executive type who flew down from New York to meet her, but he seemed hardly to know how to hold her hand, much less make babies before she gets too old for it.

And then there's Timothy, always ready to tell me about his most recent interest. Actually, this week he was much more interested in impressing me with his brand-new thirty-five millimeter Nikon camera with a long telescopic lens. He even took me out to an old abandoned, kind of classical-Greek–looking mansion in the suburbs, where he had taken a number of pictures—both of the structure and of his latest girl friend, Lolly or Cookie or something like that. I must admit that he does succeed in pulling off that sexy image like the men in the *New Yorker* camera advertisements. Or am I thinking of the old Marlboro ads? His act is so stereotyped, so obvious, so macho. For instance, he doesn't wear a T-shirt under his dental clinic smock, and after clinic hours he casually unbuttons the high neck and lets his hairy chest show. But like I say, he does look good—turns me on anyway. But his problem this week is merely how to seduce Lolly or Candy or whatever her name is with his superduper camera.

So you see, I do have a life outside of my books, despite what Jake may tell you. *I* could be a psychiatrist with the case load I carry. But that's what really confuses me. How come I seem to do fine relating to all of these people, and yet fail so miserably most of the time with Jake? Why does he seem to want to hold me away from him, at arm's length most of the time, until we're in bed, where he won't keep his hands off me? And why doesn't *he* want to talk about problems or anything else with me? Actually, to give you a little bit of credit, I do sometimes get the feeling that he is at least trying to connect, but it's usually by talking about someone else or some other couple. We've agreed that when it comes to other people's problems, we have a crystal ball; but somehow, when it is our own problems, the crystal ball is a murky, useless fog in an overturned fishbowl. As Jake says, "How is it two intelligent, relatively perceptive people like ourselves are unable to understand and work out the problems between us?" How indeed. But isn't that what we're paying *you* for?

April is right around the corner. Back to a full tennis schedule, I imagine. I'm waiting to see if this spring will be any different—kind of a quantitative test of your success with my husband. Or do you perhaps think all that tennis is a healthy outlet? I'll tell you right now that if it continues—no, wait. I've decided to give up these childish threats. But let's be reasonable this spring, shall we?

Sincerely,
JEANNE

March 28

DEAR DR. FRICKMAN,

It's a trap, all a fantastically complex, expensive trap. I finally see it all. More alluring than the Siren's song, more frustrating and more potentially destructive than the rocks of Scylla or the whirlpool of Charybdis. You analysts have a complete, closed, circular system that puts the patient at the will of your whimsical winds. You're like little gods up in the sky arguing with each other and pushing some mere human about. And I can see that the poor wanderer, my husband Jake, may be caught in this system, a victim ever as much as Odysseus, and perhaps for as long—ten years! You know, now that I think of it, if Homer hadn't written the *Odyssey* long before Freud developed his amazing circular system, I'd say that the *Odyssey* was about a man in psychoanalysis—all those dreams and crazy adventures with the analyst magically changing his shape from the terrifying, cannibalistic, one-eyed Cyclops at one session to the enchanting, seductive form of Circe at the next. And no way out of it all for the wanderer—a heroic fool who is searching for a way to control his own fate.

And then there's faithful Penelope, sitting at home weaving or some such nonsense (making macramé plant hangers, perhaps?). Does anyone ever think that she too must have a tale to tell?

Why, doctor, why is Jake so depressed, so down about everything? I simply cannot be the faithful Penelope wondering what is going on. I mean, for a while I even considered the possibility of another woman . . . that maybe he was ignoring me because he had someone else. But that's not it. I read his behavior better than that, and besides, he's too depressed to be enjoying himself.

It's you. You are that Cyclops monster and that irresistible Siren; you feast him comfortably like Calypso and then you drag him about in storms like Poseidon. I despise you for keeping him there, for making him so dependent that we have to drive back from visiting relatives at two in the morning in order not to miss an analytic session at 7:00 A.M. And yet, I find myself as dependent as he is, hopeful that you will also guide him through this strange, terrible journey, safely back to me. I hate him, I love him. I hate you, I love you. If I've learned anything through this whole odyssey, it's that one can say those two things in one breath and mean it.

Sincerely,
JEANNE

April 1

DEAR DR. FRICKMAN,

Randy called! Jake had been out three evenings in a row this week for tennis, and I hesitated only one second before accepting an invitation to have coffee. When he phoned I was angrily eating a well-overdone dinner which Jake had still not arrived home for, and I agreed to meet Randy the next morning downtown. He said he was in town to see and hear some old friends of his, musicians who were opening at some club or coffee house in center city. So I had coffee with him in a cafeteria on Broad Street (mostly because it was convenient to the subway). He met me with an affectionate, enveloping hug, as if we had known each other all our lives, as if we were childhood pals who had grown up, grown apart, and met again to discover that our lives would always be intertwined by an infinite number of spun filaments, as if we had discovered that we could almost intuitively understand each other, always know what the other was thinking or feeling about anything. It was a connection—a connection of souls, of kindred spirits—and the energy we felt between us inevitably led us to consider a physical connection as well. But I knew I couldn't handle that right now—too much of a threat to my handling of everyday reality—and we agreed to let it be. No demands, no claims, but an ever-deepening sense of responsibility. To everything there is a season.

I admit it, I admit it—I *do* feel a bit guilty—why else would I be telling *you* about it? Well there is another reason, doctor. I felt ecstatic, delighted, joyous to be with Randy, even telling him how I feel about being pregnant, about my crazy-women dissertation, about my hopes to do something really creative with my life, and listening to him tell his story about dropping out of conventional society for awhile (he lived out in Idaho in a farmhouse with some jazz musicians for over three years), about later withdrawing into his parents' apartment for nearly six months after his father had been injured in an auto accident, and about his gradual emergence back into this world (to become, it seems to me, a sensitive poet who hears a special music inside his own head). I let him do most of the talking as I listened, often fascinated. He would take any comment or question of mine and weave a tapestry of words in response. The way he reacted to my feelings about being pregnant, for example, made me come away feeling like a mythological earth mother. I listened to the story of his life, of his relationships, of his hopes, but I chose not to talk about my everyday reality, my relationship with Jake. Randy may have heard a bit already from Nancy (who can't understand why in the world I stay with Jake). Besides, the two relationships are so far apart in my psyche that it is absolutely unnecessary to talk to Randy about Jake. Yet, even though those few hours were lovely, beautiful, I now feel absolutely depressed. Why can't I talk like that to Jake? Will I *ever* be able to talk like that with Jake?

You know, it *was* different with Jake and me way back when we first met. It was all terribly romantic; we were both working at a big hotel in the Catskills on a summer vacation from college. He was a bar waiter and I waited on tables, working myself into a headache every single day trying to please those people three times a day, six days a week. (I had several psychiatrists at my tables during the course of the summer, by the way. An interesting lot, to say the least—but I'll save that story for another time.) Jake and I would meet every night after he got off work (nearly midnight most nights) and take long walks in the cool air through beautiful pine-wood paths, talking about books and ideas and philosophy and about ourselves. We used to save sugar cubes from the dining room for our favorite horse in the hotel stables, and often we warmed up over coffee or hot chocolate at an all-night diner in the little town a mile or two from the hotel. When I had a day off we'd either take a picnic and swim in a mountain stream nearby or, if it was rainy, we'd go to the hotel library—if one could call it that; it was mainly a collection of old nineteenth- and early twentieth-century novels and some volumes of poetry and history and a few books about the geography or natural environment of the surrounding area, astronomy, and insects.

Because we both lived in dormitories, segregated into men's and women's areas, of course, we sometimes dressed in several layers of warm clothes and dragged five or six blankets and a few pillows out to the woods and spent the night together—all very innocent. The only problem was that I had to be ready and presentably dressed in my starched uniform, apron, and hat at 7:00 A.M. to serve huge breakfasts to obese, pretentious people whom I learned to pity for their sedentary ways and for their demands for prunes. But not everyone was like that—and actually I got to know some wonderful people quite well over a week or two-week period; it was lovely to find those kindly types who enjoyed playing benefactor to a struggling college student. Jake had the same experience in the cocktail lounge, and we had many long talks about our "clients" and about our study of human nature, especially of the rich and the aged.

As I said, it was all much different then. We shared ideas and emotions; I thought we both were interested in discovering what other people were like, how they lived, how they thought, how they hated and loved. And I thought Jake was interested in the real person inside me—in all my selves—not only in the self that is presented to the world (for of course it is not possible to walk around with one's insides vulnerable, exposed to all).

So what has happened? Was I so wrong about Jake? So often now—partly, I suspect, because of medical school, but largely since analysis—he seems like a machine, a logical computer, able to ask questions and give answers without a tear, without a laugh, without any feeling at all. He is like a machine that has become expert at searching its own depths, its own memory banks, its own data, and then, with a low, mechanical hum, he prints out the answer with never so much as a smile. An exaggeration? Perhaps, but Jake is surely more often like this than he was before analysis. He can be absolutely oblivious to *my* tears, tirades, or teasing by merely pointing out something that sounds like, "I am not programmed to respond to that," in an emotionless tone.

But those other selves are still there inside him, doctor. I know they are, for sometimes that introspective machine breaks down and some of the data in those memory banks spring out and try to touch the world in any way possible—perhaps in anger or even rage, perhaps in a rare expression of tenderness or sympathy or love. You know what I think? Thank goodness that the machine *can* still break down, can go into dysfunction. All that looking inward must get to be such a strain. It allows little time for looking into anything else or, what's so much more important, anyone else. You will say that psychoanalysis does not seek to obliterate a man's relation to his world, that it does not propose to isolate him as a self-contained entity, but don't you see that all that self-searching just has to place a person in that very danger? Where is compassion? Where is relationship? Where is love? (I know, I know, you are not programmed to respond to that.)

I told Jake I had coffee with Randy and that we talked for a couple of hours. He only made some remark like, "I thought you were so busy that you don't have enough time to teach and write your dissertation and do housework." Good machine; computes all the available data quite well.

Sincerely,
JEANNE

April 6

DEAR DR. FRICKMAN,

You are finally making some progress—and I'm not being sarcastic, either. I've been complaining about handling our money and balancing the checkbook for at least two years, and about having to figure out those income tax forms by myself for even longer. So here I was, this year, getting all worked up about federal, state, and city taxes and fuming about how the checkbook never seems to balance when Jake marches in and announces that he is now taking over all our financial business, such as it is. Up until now he knew only how to write a check out to you—nothing about depositing or withdrawing or account numbers or drive-up windows, or how much the electricity bill is, or how much we pay for food in a month. So I have now happily handed over the whole mess to him. It's wonderful! I can see already that he doesn't give a damn about balancing it all out when the canceled checks come in the mail, but I don't even care. It is out of my hands once and for all. I'll tell you, doctor, I have the feeling that this is somehow a very large step for Jake, for us, not only in a practical way but symbolically as well. Does this mean he's responding (or you're responding?) to my pleas for him to take more responsibility here at home? God, I hope so.

I wonder—did you expect quite the opposite reaction, that I would make a protest about this? That I would become super-bitch, the controlling, castrating witch? You think that despite my complaints I really liked holding the purse strings? That I enjoy bringing in most of our income? That I find pleasure in having had Jake so dependent on me for even pocket money? I sometimes read such feelings in Jake—oh, not through direct discourse of course, but through direct intercourse, if you know what I mean . . . that he tries to prove to me, there in the final frontier, that *he* is in charge despite the economic structure of our lives. And you know, I'm denying all that about being a bitch-witch-castrater, and yet I'm half admitting it—only to you, of course—because I think it *has* been true that I liked having Jake be emotionally dependent on me. But you know, it's only because I want to be dependent on him, to be taken care of, not to be this very independent self all the time. Am I making sense? You're an analyst; surely you will understand this vague, ambivalent kind of expression? I want—*interaction!*

So! Again I congratulate you on this big step, on Jake's taking over the mighty checkbook and all that this might imply. Sometimes, just once in awhile, I begin to think that this is not all such a waste of money. However this new development came about, I'm grateful. Thank Freud that I don't have to fill out those tedious tax forms ever again!

Regards,
JEANNE

April 16

DEAR DR. FRICKMAN,

I'm sitting on a green, wooden, slatted bench on the side of the tennis court as I write. Jake has urged (almost *forced*) me to come and watch him instead of staying home to grade papers or plan lectures. He can't stand to play with me now that he's so good at it, but he seems to want me to come and sit here so he won't feel so guilty about leaving the house. Is this some little solution the two of you worked out together—to have me sitting here, the adoring wife, a passive part of the scenery here at the park? This is definitely not my style, although it is rather more pleasant (if slower) to grade these freshman themes here with some interesting distractions.

For example, I've been studying these bodies (all male at the moment—the theory is that the women have all day to play and so should clear the courts evenings and weekends), bodies aged from about seventeen to about sixty and economic statuses from struggling student (that's Jake in the cutoffs and surgical top) to upper middle class (the older man there in the always-clean, white everything who brings a clean white towel to wipe his forehead and a thermos of water for after the games). I'm trying to figure out if I can get turned on just by concentrating on the bodies—the hairy legs, bulging middles or slim waistlines, flat or rounded asses, the sweaty backs, long arms, wide shoulders. No, I find I need to look at more than bodies; I need to look at their faces, their haircuts (those who try to hide their baldness by combing their other hair over it are exposed when they play tennis; others, it becomes obvious, use hair spray), and especially at their expressions as they serve, hit, and miss. Some look alternately triumphant and dejected. Others, and Jake is a master at this, manage to look quite cool whether they have aced a serve or have slammed at a ball right up close to the net and had it come down on their own side instead of their opponent's. Somehow, that coolness, that emotional detachment is much more attractive to me than the genuine grins and frowns on the other type of men. Now, why should that be? Why should these controlled, competitive, closed-book types be more attractive to me than those who allow their emotions to show in their facial expressions and their bodies? I certainly would expect myself and most women to be out there smiling, swinging arms, or jumping with excitement when doing well, or making faces when doing poorly.

Anyway, as I said, it's an interesting distraction. But I have *so* much work to do, and being pregnant is making me feel extremely tired. And Adam asked me to take over his classes for a week while he's in the hospital for tests (his nervous stomach is acting up again). I stopped in to see him there today since I had to see my ob-gyn in the medical building right next to the hospital. Funny thing about that—Adam was obviously surprised and pleased to see me there; he is very sensitive and I can read emotions and feelings on his face as clearly as if he spoke about each feeling. I hardly look pregnant and hadn't yet told Adam, but today seemed like a good time since I could explain why I was at the medical center.

Well, was *I* surprised at his reaction. He was shocked at first, shocked with a touch of pity—as if I were an unmarried fifteen-year-old who had been naïve or negligent enough to become pregnant. I was confused by this and hastened to explain that I was *happy* about this turn of events, that we had indeed even *planned* it. Adam, brilliant, sensitive philosopher that he is, tried to hide his sense of ... well, I guess it was betrayal and anger, as if I had somehow been fooling him or deliberately lying to him. But he wouldn't talk about it—nothing beyond the mere conventions of "Well, congratulations then" and "When is it due?" So I mumbled a few conventional words myself about hoping he'd feel better soon and hoping they'll find out what's wrong, etc.—and got up to leave. Then he asked me casually, without looking at me (very unusual for Adam): "What about your dissertation? Will you be able to finish it?" By then I decided that *I* was angry so I said, "Sure," and walked out. The nerve of men!

It's getting dark; I can barely see to write this letter any longer, and Jake and a few others are still straining their eyes to see those damnable balls. Narcissists all, performing their rituals until they go blind. If it *was* your idea for me to sit here watching, I thank you for one day of distraction, but it really will not do. I have important things to accomplish back at my desk. And watching Jake play hours of tennis is not my idea of a relationship.

Sorry, doc, you'll just have to do better than that.

Nice try, though.

As always,
JEANNE

April 23

DEAR DR. FRICKMAN,

Last night my women's book group met. We discussed a book of short stories by a contemporary writer—Grace Paley's *The Little Disturbances of Man*. Have you read it? The "little disturbances" are the problems from which men and women suffer every day, just because they are men and women, because they are different from each other, because they love and hate. It brought together many of the vague thoughts and feelings I've had about people and their problems, "people" meaning my small universe of friends, family, and acquaintances; including, of course, Jake and me. It became obvious to me as I sat there that there are problems, real, concrete problems. Like my old high school friend, Sally, who wrote to me recently from Canada. After a terrible first marriage, then a heart-rending broken engagement, she finally married a third man with hopes of beginning a happier life—only to have him become seriously ill on their honeymoon. Now he is lingering in some Canadian hospital in the very dubious nets of multiple sclerosis. And a friend of mine who is a physical therapist just told me about a visit to an unmarried, uneducated woman on welfare who gave birth to twins three months ago; they were born with congenital rubella, and already all kinds of physical and developmental abnormalities are being recognized. And these are only from my tiny sphere of significance. Just think of all the very real, very terrible problems of so many people—like the children starving or undernourished in Biafra or any number of other places; like the old people living out isolated, boring existences in costly nursing homes right here in this city; like the blind and maimed and psychologically damaged millions who have lived through a war firsthand, close-up, who have watched loved ones suffer or die, who have had to place their children aboard helicopters hoping to save them from uncertain horrors . . . and then have never seen them again; and others who have fought to survive in sadistic camps where people were treated worse than animals and then put into ovens like potatoes. *These* are problems, real problems that seem only to whimper for one's recognition, empathy, compassion when one is caught up in the trivial problems of day-to-day existence.

And then there are the other kind of problems: the problems we make for ourselves, the problems we scream about because we are "unhappy," because our own little worlds have been disturbed, have failed to give us the maximum of pleasure and the minimum of pain. Of course these are real problems in their own way, and I do believe such problems deserve recognition and empathy and compassion too. But we need to keep them in perspective; we can't allow them to ruin our lives. Take Jake. He is a physically healthy, attractive, intelligent, ambitious man who had loving parents and grandparents, who received a good education, and who is now very close to becoming, presumably, a wealthy surgeon, a man whose profession will give him a respected place in our society as well as a great deal of personal satisfaction. Though I should perhaps be more humble, I will add that he also has the advantage of being married to me—a reasonable person to be married to, and a good partner in the final account, I think—and we're even expecting our very own child, a part of us, a being to give to, a being who may give us our immortality. Now I ask you: Is this a man with a problem, a man who needs to pay someone to listen to the vicissitudes of his everyday life five days a week for several years?

Jake, and my friend Evelyn, and David, and Michael—and me —we all have problems, problems that can *seem* earthshaking and that do cry out for resolution. But such problems must be recognized for what they are, in the right perspective. They are "the little disturbances of man." Evelyn came to my office in tears this week because she finally went out with a man she really liked. She saw him twice, was swept off her feet, and was beginning to hear wedding bells. And then he didn't call her again. (He must have heard them too.) And then there's David, who's beginning to worry about what he will do about his passionate liaison with a dental hygiene student when his fiancée arrives from Arizona in July. And Michael. Michael has always found me a good listener for his many complaints, whether about making dentures, suffering with asthma and allergies, or losing a prospective girl to Timothy's charms. Michael is *plagued* with the little disturbances of man (although from what little I've read, Freud would blame it on his mother). Today he knocked on my door, just as I was sitting down to plan this week's lectures, to ask me if I would please stitch up the seam of his clinic gown. Helpless, just helpless, I was thinking, when I realized from his expression that he had another reason for coming over, that he needed to talk about something. Michael's woes are never short ones, so I put all my papers aside, got out my thread and needle, and put the coffee on. Such preparations made him comfortable enough to tell me his latest all-consuming problem—sexual impotence. Why me? A married, experienced woman with practical advice—is that what he thinks? Lord, if he only knew. Or am I supposed to bolster his ego? Or simply give sympathy and compassion? So I listened; I kept looking down at the seam, at the needle going in and out of the material, then looking up briefly now and then, mumbling a word or two of encouragement or sympathy, simply trying to reflect what he was feeling. And finally I suggested one of the psychological counselors I know of down at school, since Michael would be eligible for free counseling as a student.

This is *it*. This is the world and these are its problems. We all have them and we do need help, sometimes from a friend, sometimes from a spouse, and sometimes even from a stranger— I'm willing to admit this much: even from a stranger whom we pay to listen and give some expert advice. But we must recognize these problems for what they are, *little disturbances*. They shouldn't be life shattering, not for people like us with so many resources right within ourselves or very close by either in friends or institutions. It is when these little disturbances receive too much emphasis—as in the five-day-a-week introspection of analysis—that they become all-consuming and make simple solutions almost impossible. If Jake could just turn some of that energy spent talking to you and thinking about himself to some more practical outlets—creative or cultural or social—I really think he'd be much better off.

Why, why do I argue with you like this? Because you are a spider and Jake is the fly, and I can't get him out of that web. Yet another of the little disturbances of man.

Sincerely,
JEANNE DANIELS

May 2

DEAR DR. FRICKMAN,

Perusing an article in a medical journal last night (while waiting for the hamburgers to finish broiling), I came across this quotation from a personal communication by Sigmund Freud: "Fools write papers that are autobiographical; wiser men confine their confessions to their analysts." That made me feel more than a bit self-conscious about writing and sending these letters to you, for of course you are not my analyst. And yet, without ever having met you during this past year and a half or so, I somehow feel that we do know each other, or rather, that you know me—at least a little. Oh, not only from these letters, but from our shared intimacy with my husband. As you must know, I used to ask him often about what he said about me during his analytic hour. He always made a point of telling me I was of little importance, that he was there to discuss *him*, not me. But I think I'm only beginning to believe that now. He really does have a life apart from me. A lonely thought, huh? Sometimes, Dr. Frickman, I feel that there is somehow a bond between us, that we both have an interest in seeing a change in this man, my husband.

But then, on the other hand, we compete, you and I. He is there talking to you—exclusively to you—for a full fifty minutes five days a week, week after week, month after month (and I shudder to mention year after year). Between his analysis, his studying, his patients, and his tennis obsession, I am lucky to get his exclusive attention for ten minutes within a period of three days. Why, I ask myself, why does he want to talk so much to that doctor and so little to me? This all reminds me of our courtship days when he was still a practicing Catholic (before his conversion to Sigmund Freudism, that is) when he used to go to confession on Friday evening after a full week of medical school classes. At that time I used to ask him what he confessed to the priest in that absurd little black telephone booth and he used to answer me with much the same tone of irritation and secrecy. And I used to think, damn the priest (obviously I'm not Catholic), who has this hold over him. And now you, doctor. Now you are the priest, the man who sees but is not observed, the man who hears all confessions but speaks not one iota of his own.

The close sanctity of the confessional booth is now the sacredness of a luxurious leather sofa in a room with a view. And the same hold is there too, father—I mean doctor! But alas. No penance. No "Our Fathers" or "Hail Marys" on one's knees out in the waiting room. You have no such quick-healing powers, no formulas for instant forgiveness. ("Pray for us, father Freud, for we have sinned and are most grievously guilty . . ." No—that leaves one kind of cold, doesn't it?) Yours, however, is a much greater strategy of power, a more insightful and more Machiavellian technique. You send him home hurting; yes, hurting. "The hour is up," says the great high priest, and the poor sinner is left to his own depression, which he must then carry home, for where else can one safely unload such a burden?

So. Fool shall I be, doctor, a fool writing autobiographical letters to you; but at least I'm out of your omnipotent control. Why do you let him—or make him—get so depressed, so wrapped up in himself and his problems? Be a little kind. Hear our prayer, O Doctor, have mercy upon us. Amen.

JEANNE

May 12

DEAR DR. FRICKMAN,

It's Sunday morning, ten o'clock. Jake is out playing tennis. I have a great deal of work to get done, especially if I am to work on my dissertation today, but I'm feeling rather lazy sitting here in our living room amongst the dirty dishes and congealing remains of a dinner party we had last night—a beef fondue for nine of us around our yellow telephone spool. I hate to get started on the cleanup and then on grading all those freshman themes that I promised to hand back by Wednesday. I like to sit here thinking about this baby growing inside me, to think it has eyelashes and toenails and every-thing already. So I'm putting all that work off for a little while and writing to you instead. This has certainly become quite a habit, hasn't it? Indeed, it would feel very strange to me to quit writing to you now.

Anyway! I thought you might be interested in hearing about our dinner party since both your patient and many of my friends-with-problems were there. I'm feeling pleased with myself this morning as I realize that I may have instigated the beginning of a resolution to two of my friends' problems—Michael's impotence and Evelyn's loneliness. Oh, not that this was conscious on my part; I am fully prepared to let my unconscious or whatever take credit. After all, I simply invited people, almost a last-minute thing actually, whom I thought Jake and I would enjoy having. We had Sydney and Mandy, who can always be counted on for excellent anecdotes and conversation—Sydney always on topics of law and politics and Mandy either on what she is presently teaching or on comic domestic events that sometimes make Sydney turn red or purple. I also invited Timothy and his date, Lolly. Neither one said much at all, but they provided a kind of sexual focus, since Timothy was constantly rubbing her legs or stroking her hair while she just sat there looking beautiful. Jake and David talked some about school, comparing the science courses of dental and medical schools, and the three of us along with Sydney and Mandy also had a long argument about the meaning of consciousness. (Actually, Jake hates the very topic and was furious with me for bringing it up.)

Michael made us all laugh from time to time with his dry one-liners, which he injects very cleverly into serious discourse. It didn't take me long to realize, however, that his best audience was Evelyn, who was looking particularly well last evening, glowing even, and who seemed fascinated by Michael—good old chronic complainer Michael! I had never even thought of introducing them to each other, hadn't even paired them in my imagination when I invited them to dinner.

Now that I think of it, they may be just perfect for one another. Michael's real interests are in chemistry, and he has recently decided to apply to a doctoral chemistry program after dental school —to do research in and teach chemistry instead of working on teeth. I heard him talking to Evelyn about all that while we were having our rather heated discussion about the meaning of human consciousness (as opposed to machines and animals, for example), and before I knew it, they were deep into a discussion of chemistry that was sparked by Evelyn's interest in medieval alchemy. Doesn't it make just perfect sense? I feel like I have fit together the key pieces in some cosmic puzzle. The more I think about it, the more I think that they may just be meant for each other. We'll see. . . . I feel sure that Michael will at least ask her out, and I feel quite confident that she will no longer need to pay for newspaper ads. Michael does indeed need *someone*—mother or wife—to sew on his buttons and to pat him on the back when things are not going well and to adore him as if he were the only man on earth. Evelyn can do all that.

Well? What do you think? Do I have the makings of a good psychiatrist? Oh, not that I'm really thinking of competing with you for such a place; I'm quite happy to practice from where I am, kind of a sideline to my real interest, literature. But I think I'm gaining some insight into how it must feel to be on *that* side of the couch, so to speak. It seems to me that from your unseen, basically unheard, post out of the patient's sight, you could very easily get a complex of some sort, a God complex I mean. On a more realistic level, that would mean that you could easily turn into an egomaniac. Doesn't that scare you? That intimate contact with the absolute inner selves of other people . . . the feeling that you can help direct those selves, that you can help them make a new shape in time and space? You know, to me that seems a great burden. And it scares me to think that you, a man I do not know at all, have seen the insides of my husband, Jake, exposed—like the workings of a watch might be to a jeweler. And you, the watch mender, poring over each detail, each gear, cleaning out each speck of dust, trying to determine what makes this particular watch tick, or not tick, as may be the case. And the outcome? It cannot affect only that watch, for there are others who orient themselves to the time and the workings of that watch.

Well, I really hadn't meant to get into these metaphors and analogies again. And anyway, your treatment is not as exact as the work of a watch mender. You have only theories; you cannot *really* know all the inner workings of a person. I just hope that you, and all your psychoanalysts, remember that. Ah—the dirty dishes and my ungraded themes are calling. Back to the more mundane affairs of this world.

Sincerely,
JEANNE

May 20

DEAR DR. FRICKMAN,

Today is a milestone in my life. Today is the last straw. Today is the last day, the very last day that I shall ever do *anything* for Jake —your childish, self-centered, insensitive patient! Sometimes I really don't see how you can stand him! Psychoanalysis is only making him more demanding and less giving. He is Ptolemy at the center of his universe, insisting that the rest of us revolve around him. I do so much for him—and he only becomes more ungrateful. Today was just too much to bear. Last night he convinced me to drive today (after teaching) out to Coopersville to buy him a new kick pedal for the Kawasaki. I no longer ride the motorcycle, now that I'm pregnant, but as Jake pointed out: Since he gives me the car (a ten-year-old Mercury that we bought for $350) so I don't have to take the bus and subway, he really needs the cycle to get to school so *he* doesn't have to take the bus and subway. Whether or not that makes sense, he convinced me that I should do him that favor. I mentioned that I had wanted to go to the store to buy some new sandals. He said I'd still have time for that *and* since I'd be at the shopping center, how about buying him some new sneakers. Here, let me write this out in dialogue. It's really too much to believe:

ME: *Me,* buy *your* sneakers? You mean at the supermarket or what?

JAKE: I want good Jack Purcells. They have them in the Florsheim store up at the shopping center.

ME: Nobody buys sneakers for someone else! You have to try them on.

JAKE: Oh come on, Jeanne, I need new sneakers for tennis. Just get the same size I have now—my old ones are up in the bedroom.

ME: They are not. They stank so much that I put them out on the balcony.

JAKE: Well, just take them and have the guy measure them.

ME: You're kidding.

JAKE: What's wrong with that? It'll only take you a few minutes. They're just sneakers—not jock straps.

ME: Well, I don't want to take them. Don't you know your size anyway? And why don't you just go get them yourself if it only takes a few minutes?

JAKE: Please Jeanne? [*Pleading tone*] I don't have time to go up there and you're going anyway and I need them for a tournament this weekend.

ME: A tournament?

JAKE: At Elkins Park Courts. I'm going to play my first round real early before work on Saturday morning—and if I win I'll play again on Sunday. You don't want me in a tournament at Elkins Park in holey, smelly sneakers, do you?

ME: Oh, I can't believe I'm doing this. I'll get them, but can't you just tell me your size?

JAKE: [*With impatience now*] Just have the guy measure my old ones!

Well—anyway, I finally agreed to buy the kick pedal *and* his sneakers, and it took up my whole afternoon and I got a headache because I had a hard time finding the motorcycle garage out there in the boondocks. And the mechanic asked me which size kick pedal. Jake never told me I would have to know which size, and I hadn't brought the old one. I was pretty sure of the year and size of the cycle so he was able to figure it out from a parts list. But I still felt like a dummy, standing in that dirty garage with its nudie calendars and very sweaty mechanics, in my pink maternity smock (yes, I've started wearing maternity clothes!) asking for a kick pedal the size of which I had not the slightest idea.

Of course that was nothing compared to walking into the Florsheim shoe store an hour later with two sneakers smelling vaguely of the Jean Naté I had splashed on them, but smelling mostly of foot rot. I could *not* bring myself to ask the man to actually measure them. He handled them gingerly as he looked in vain to find the size on the inside; finally he just guessed and put the new ones sole to sole with the old ones. It was difficult to tell but they looked like size eleven.

When Jake arrived home later this evening, he grunted at the kick pedal (in approval I imagine) and then tried on the sneakers. Too big. Half a size too big.

JAKE: Jeanne! [*Imperious voice from the bedroom*] What size are these?

ME: [*Stalling*] Look inside them—or on the box.

JAKE: Did you have the salesman measure my old ones?

ME: The size was rubbed off inside. Boy, did I feel silly carrying those smelly old things into the store.

JAKE: Did you tell him to *measure* them?

ME: Well, he did measure the new ones against the old ones.

JAKE: You mean, he *didn't* measure the old ones?

ME: I guess it would have been better to go yourself. Are they too big or too small?

JAKE: Jeanne! Why didn't you tell him to measure them like I told you to do? You didn't tell him, did you?

ME: I told him I wanted the same size. He looked inside and there was no size so he brought some out and measured them against the old ones.

JAKE: But why didn't you just tell him to *measure* the old ones on the measuring plate?

This went on ad nauseum for almost twenty minutes, at which time it turned into Jake yelling and me crying. And then I started yelling about this dumb analysis and how it makes him believe he is some kind of imperial wizard. And do you believe that two hours later— by that time we had calmed and I was busy with my dissertation— he casually asked me to buy a gift for his mother's birthday? I do absolutely refuse. His *own* mother, who must have done all this stuff for him before he found me.

You *must* discourage this behavior. I can't stand it anymore. I don't want him to depend on me for everything. And I want to be a little more dependent on him—especially now that I'm pregnant and my body seems to be changing so much, so fast, and I'm so tired, and I feel so vulnerable. Like when Timothy said to me today in a really unfriendly tone, "So you're really gonna have a kid, huh?" And then he looked down at my body: "Well, it'll ruin your figure, kid." Idiot! Idiots—all of them—Timothy and Jake and you.

This is *it*, I tell you. I'm nobody's mother yet, and nobody's property either. I'm going to be my own self from now on. If that makes me a "bitch," fine, I'm a bitch. I don't care.

JEANNE DANIELS

May 28

DEAR DR. FRICKMAN,

Don't think I'm writing to apologize for last week's letter. I meant it, every word. From now on I'm going to be angry when I'm angry. And happy when I'm happy, and sad when I'm sad, and enthusiastic when I'm enthusiastic, and depressed when I'm depressed. No more covering up, no more fitting in with Jake's moods. You know, I really thought for all this long time that it was me, my moods, that determined how things went at our house. What a relief to discover what I should have realized ages ago, that it is (mainly) Jake's moods that determine the tone and tenor of our relationship. If he's tense, depressed, angry (from dealing with professors or tests or patients or lack of sleep) then he is a most unpleasant person here at home. Often. And when things are going well, when he's been able to relax with a few hours of tennis or a macho movie on Friday night, he's a much warmer, affectionate man—indeed, almost a totally different person, more the person I thought I married, and then everything seems fine.

Yesterday was my birthday—twenty-six. Jake had overnight duty at the hospital, but miraculously he remembered to get me a card and a gift on the way home the day before (I know because he was late and walked in with my present in a bag). I was touched by his gifts—some really lovely earrings and a beautiful book about the prenatal development of the child with lots of almost mystical-looking photographs. I was especially pleased since Jake has so far taken little interest, or so it would seem, in this pregnancy. After the initial excitement, he has said almost nothing and has certainly not been my idea of a solicitous husband. Here I am asking him

about names, telling him what I've been reading about natural
child-birth and about breast feeding and about infant development
—and he seems bored, annoyed almost, and says he just can't get
into all of that *yet*. So it was beautiful for him to get that book for
me. He gave it to me in the morning before he left for school and
said a few tender-funny words about our future tennis player. I
actually sat down and cried when he left. I wouldn't have expected
such a birthday in a thousand years. Last year he brought home a
card and a bag of candies which he bought at the candy store at the
top of the subway steps. To think he really planned a little ahead
this year and tried so hard to please me. So you see, even though I'm
not apologizing to you, you are definitely moving off my shit list.
You may actually be bringing out his better side after all. But I've
learned not to draw any rash conclusions or raise any false hopes.
Sigh.

Anyway, yesterday was a wonderful day, even if Jake did have
overnight duty. I received a few little gifts down at school: an
anthology of women's poetry from Adam, a card and a box of
peanut butter cups (my favorite) from Nancy, and six assorted tiny
tins of loose tea from Evelyn, and my mother sent me a card with
a twenty-dollar bill. The guys next door invited me for dinner;
David even stuck candles in the lasagne, and I had such a good time
I couldn't really feel badly about getting older. When I finally went
home at around nine-thirty, I didn't feel like working on my dissertation or planning next week's lecture, so I gave myself a bit of a
gift—free reading time to finish reading Iris Murdoch's *Under the
Net*. Its philosophical undercurrents made me feel that it was somehow very appropriate for me, a woman of twenty-six, alone after a
full day of people and thinking about age and the future and all the
things that one's birthday celebration evokes. I underlined this passage thinking of you, of Jake, of myself, of everyone's problems and
projects and preoccupations:

And as I looked down now on the crowds in Oxford Street and stroked
Mar's head I felt neither happy nor sad, only rather unreal, like a man shut
in a glass. Events stream past us like these crowds and the face of each is
seen only for a minute. What is urgent is not urgent for ever but only
ephemerally. All work and all love, the search for wealth and fame, the

search for truth, life itself, are made up of moments which pass and become nothing. Yet through this shaft of nothings we drive onward with that miraculous vitality that creates our precarious habitations in the past and the future. So we live; a spirit that broods and hovers over the continual death of time, the lost meaning, the unrecaptured moment, the unremembered face, until the final chop that ends all our moments and plunges that spirit back into the void from which it came.

Isn't it wonderful? Doesn't it make you want to burn your couch, tell your patients to go home, throw away your books, put on some music, and begin appreciating what beauty and vitality exists in this world and in each of us? Well, perhaps it can't do all that, but it sure makes a good deal more sense to me than. . . . Oh, why bother? Actually I'm praising you today. Jake is trying very hard, and I suspect you really do have something to do with that— and I thank you.

> Gratefully,
> Jeanne Daniels

June 4

DEAR DR. FRICKMAN,

Dear Big Brother would perhaps be closer to what I'm feeling as I write this. The Big Brother of *1984*, I mean, not some kindly man who signs up to give companionship to some lonely orphan in the big cities. I know it sounds paranoid, but you, doctor, are indeed a kind of Big Brother, with a good view of any and all aspects of our lives. "Big Brother is watching you." What really struck me about that book *(1984)* and what similarly strikes me about analysis is the relentlessness of it all. There is virtually no rest from it or from its influence. Even the private domain of one's dreams is utterly vulnerable. Now, after seventeen months of Jake's analysis, I find your Freudian system practically a part of our lives, like a Bible would be to religious fundamentalists, like *Das Kapital* to revolutionaries, like Machiavelli's *The Prince* to a monarch. And there is certainly a good amount of doublethink and doublespeak going on. That is, nothing is ever what it seems, according to Jake, at any rate.

He has labels for everyone, for any kind of behavior, for any event. The simplest acts or words or gestures must be analyzed and labeled. As I've mentioned before, my friend Timothy has a voluptuous new girl friend every couple of weeks or so, because—according to Jake—of an "unresolved Oedipal"; and the reason he has chosen dentistry is because of "castration anxiety." The depression of my friend Janice (which has caused her to lose fifteen pounds, miss taking her master's exam, and cry at the drop of a hat) is actually a form of hostility. Old Mrs. Van Ness, whom we often see outside on her knees with her hands in the dirt pulling up weeds from her beautiful flower garden, is actually acting out her repressed childhood desire to play with feces. And when I mentioned (all right, complained) about low-back pain the other day after scrubbing the kitchen and bathroom floors, he told me that it was a neurotic symptom.

The one that *really* gets me, though, is the fear-wish routine. This seems to come up often for some reason. For example, last Friday night we had plans to attend a cocktail party at my modern literature professor's home. Jake *had* to play tennis first (Freud forbid I should deny my husband his exercise; any attempt I make to modify such activity is directly labeled castrating). The cocktail party was at 6:30. I began getting angry when he wasn't home by 6:00; at 6:30 I was straining to hear the sound of his motorcycle (which *I* have secretly labeled the "penis machine"); at 7:00 I was getting worried, looking up emergency numbers, wondering whom to call. At 7:30 I realized it was really too dark for playing tennis anymore, and I became extremely anxious—tears, even—afraid that something must have happened to Jake on that motorcycle. He came in a few minutes later—nonchalant—asking what time we had to leave for the party, opening the frig and looking for something to eat. I tried to explain to him, between his bites of leftover peach pie and his concoction of cottage cheese with garlic salt, that I had been frantic with worry—that I had feared the motorcycle had at last done him in. (I *had* to be dramatic to make him understand.) He laughed (at which point I poured his glass of iced tea into the sink) and seemed altogether quite amused at seeing me dressed for a cocktail party and screaming rather hysterically.

When we were both calmer, in the car on the way home from the party several hours later, I tried to tell him again how worried, how fearful I had been. He says with that slick little grin of his, "Ah —but was it the *fear* or the *wish?*" He delivers these questions with all the clarity and smugness of the Cheshire Cat, as if he were making some beatific revelation.

That must be what you do to him. Is it, doctor? I mean, make these succinct little "interpretations" or "confrontations" so fears become wishes and, I suppose, so black becomes white and hot, cold? What an absolute, idiotic system. I have no doubt that if a patient came to you relatively healthy, he or she would have to leave it quite the opposite after such treatment. For this, I tell myself, for this I have no furniture and no new clothes and no eating out. Just vacations spent in a tent in an old sleeping bag.

Ugh!

Ever,
JEANNE DANIELS

June 16

DEAR DR. FRICKMAN,

You know, sometimes I wonder if Jake even sees me as a person anymore. He is on overnight duty again at the hospital, and it's nearly midnight, and he hasn't even called me. Oh, not that that's a big deal—calling me, I mean. I know how busy things can get and how anxious he gets about doing everything right to help those people. But I thought he would call me sometime today or tonight because I was feeling so depressed this morning and because I had these shooting pains in my right thigh. He did ask me, before he left, what was the matter and if *that* was what was making me feel depressed (he's picking up a very practical, clinical approach) and then gave me a perfunctory hug before rushing off to see *you* for fifty minutes. I can't hope to compete. Did he even mention me, I wonder? Did he tell you that I'm *never* sick, *never* seriously hurt or in pain, and *never* depressed or anxious or otherwise upset either?

Never—according to him anyway. It is true that I rarely am any of those things, but if I do have a pain or feel nauseous or express some anxiety, he pretends I'm a child begging for attention. I am not to be indulged one little bit; if he ignores my complaints, they'll go away. And the same goes for asking for help with some household task or shopping. The argument is that pregnancy is a normal state; a pregnant woman is not an invalid; the women in China work in the fields right through labor and go back to work within hours after delivery.

I don't want to be so strong, so independent, such a sparkling example. Don't get me wrong. I don't expect to be treated like a princess who mopes in bed all day. I don't even mind the grocery shopping or the vacuuming, but why can't Jake find some time to listen to how I feel? We had talked so much before about having a child and he seemed so excited about it, and now . . . he seems to want to back away from me, not to hear about what it feels like, how I'm feeling. Why? I don't understand. Do you? Do you know why he behaves like this toward me? Don't you think it would help things if I could know?

Two days ago I felt our baby *move*. I had thought I might have felt it before, but this time I was very sure. And I've felt it again since. I could hardly wait to tell Jake. He smiled and quickly calculated the age of the fetus in weeks and said yes, I should be feeling it move by now. Pooh! Who needs a clinical opinion? I was so disappointed. I wanted him to say, Oh, let me feel it too, how wonderful, just think. . . . I know he's a doctor (almost) and has seen plenty of pregnant women and several babies being born. But does that mean that I, his own wife, am to be treated like a statistic? I am a woman who has a little human being stirring within her—his wife, his child. Am I just being overly sensitive about all this? Other people seem so much more interested in my pregnancy. Nancy, for example, is so very supportive. She and Brook took me out to dinner the other night (Jake had overnight duty at the hospital) to celebrate the end of the semester. They are leaving next week for a month in Italy. We talked about my child and about children and careers and what having a child means to a woman and to a man, and other similar topics, all through dinner, from cucumber soup through cheesecake. And it wasn't all me. They were very interested, asked a lot of questions, even wanted to help choose a name. (What do you think of Morgan for a boy?) They both wanted to know what it physically feels like to be pregnant, and how I feel mentally and emotionally about it, too. Thank goodness for friends.

So summer is just about here. And Jake begins his last year of medical school. I'm a bit behind on my dissertation writing schedule, but I'll only be teaching one course in summer school—just enough to get a summer fellowship—so I'm still hoping to be nearly done at least by the time this baby arrives. Jake doesn't understand my anxiety to get it done, which means he doesn't understand how much it means to me to be someone in my own right, not just the doctor's wife. As you can probably tell, I'm feeling rather in despair today at this whole situation. Indeed, lately I've even begun to wish I had my own analyst to go and talk to. On days like this I can really feel what a relief it must be to talk to an objective observer. Although writing these letters is definitely helpful to me in some way, the utter lack of response from you makes them, probably, an exercise in futility. Nevertheless, I guess Adam and Nancy and these letters to you will have to do for now.

Sincerely,
Jeanne

June 20

Dear Dr. Frickman,

I do absolutely retract the impulsive closing statements in my last letter. In *no way* do I want to waste my time talking to an analyst, pouring out my life in its entirety of trivia—and paying for it, no less! Such fantasies grow out of my vulnerable spots—like being so disappointed in Jake's attitude. I figure it's a matter of taking a practical viewpoint, of dealing with the realities. I've learned this from Jake who, I suppose, may get it from you. I agree that it is fine to sit down and consider the reality of the situation and the alternative actions one may take, but such a view can also be very cold, hard, and unfeeling. One loses something. At any rate,

I now can say (a bit more hardened, a bit more coldly each time): OK, this is Jake, this is how he reacts, I may or may not be able to make him react differently to me, but right now I can only worry about my own feelings and attitudes. I am delighted, mystified, a bit frightened, content, anxious, exalted, depressed; at any given moment I could be *any* of these things depending on whether I'm dealing with my pregnancy, my dissertation, my future career, my friends, my family, my marital relationship. So let Jake's attitude be his problem. (Ah, if I could only remember that when he walks in depressed and ruins my good mood.) So—no analyst for me; one invisible, all-pervasive analyst is enough in this family.

Not that I don't believe in psychiatry generally, you know. Michael has been to a university counselor, a clinical psychologist, about his problem, and he seems to feel the guy may really be able to help him or *is* helping him or something. (Thank heavens he did not feel the need to tell me the details.) But from what little he said, I assume the doctor is using a behavioral technique, not digging endlessly back into his past to reveal his domineering, overprotective mother or his ineffective father or his jealousy of an older sister, or anything like that. Here's a problem. Here's how to solve it. Practical solutions to real problems. Why can't *you* be like that? What do you analysts have against speedy solutions anyway? Those behaviorists, from what I've read, really focus in on specific problems and go ahead and solve them without further ado. Deathly afraid of dogs? You'll learn to let even a Great Dane slobber over you and enjoy it. Have an eight-year-old throwing ten tantrums a day for sweets? He'll soon be eating brussels sprouts and wearing a halo. No couch, no rambling on and on. Practical solutions to *real* problems. Of course, for the doctor it might mean more work looking for new patients and a reduction in economic rewards if patients get well in two or three months instead of two or three years.

At any rate, Michael seems to be improving, but he still hasn't asked Evelyn out. I'm sure they hit it off at my dinner party, but I suspect Michael is trying to work out his problem first.

This is not simply a retraction letter. There is another reason for my writing (although by now this has become such a habit, almost a necessity, that I don't much feel the need for *reasons* to write to you). I've been reading up a bit more on dreams, always a fascinating subject to me. Despite my objections to your long, drawn-out process of treatment, I do really have great faith in the unconscious mind. I've learned, in writing many scholarly papers during these years of graduate school, and now in my dissertation too, that there is definitely something else besides one's conscious, thinking mind at work. I mean, one puzzles and puzzles over all the material one has gathered, and it may all look hopeful but devastatingly disorganized, and one may have no idea how to fit it together. Then, perhaps after a night's sleep, or during a tennis game, or while scrubbing the floor, *click,* an idea, an organizing principle of research seems to crash together in a harmonious crescendo—like a golden sun coming up over the ocean, suddenly making everything radiant, shining. I like to think of the unconscious as a kind of enormous, inexhaustible power that one can learn to harness, at times, for conscious purposes—like writing papers and, I assume, composing music or poetry and other such creative acts. (I have had many talks about this with Adam, who writes poetry from time to time, and he quite agrees about the strange surge of the unconscious.)

Anyway, it was not my intention to give you a laywoman's view of the unconscious; I wanted to tell you about an interesting dream I had this week. I wrote it down so I wouldn't forget. As I say, I've been reading up on dreams a bit—about manifest content and latent content and so on—but I still find it difficult, though fascinating, to interpret a dream. I must say, Adam and I had a good time with this one: I dreamed I had a twin sister, an identical twin. One of us was quite fat and growing fatter, the other was thin—quite pretty, attractive—but growing thinner and thinner, as if suffering from anorexia nervosa. The strange thing is, I can't tell you *which twin* I was in the dream. Sometimes I thought I was the fat one blowing up like a balloon, feeling swollen out of all identity, and sometimes I was the thin one who could no longer eat, who was shrinking out of all identity. In the dream, my father came into the room where we both were, and he ignored the fat twin and showed his great disappointment over the thin twin (me at the moment). "Jeanne," he said, "don't dissolve yourself like this." I was thinking about that strange word, *dissolve,* when *you* walked in with Jake. (And suddenly my father disappeared. I thought he might have turned into you when I wasn't looking.) Then you told Jake that *this* twin (the fat one, who was now me) was OK. You told him that if he'd just take her to the hospital (I think it was the hospital), all would be well. Jake put his arms right around me and gave me a wonderful hug. I woke up wanting to have sex, so we did, and it was lovely. Like I said, I certainly do not underestimate the power of the unconscious mind. We need our fantasies both sleeping and waking. Now what, I wonder, might I have learned from such a dream if I were talking to my own analyst instead of filling up blank pages to you? Adam and I had a good laugh about your showing up in my dreams again. Quite the intruder. I can't even get away from you in my sleep.

Sincerely,
JEANNE

June 28

DEAR DR. FRICKMAN,

Michael has finally asked Evelyn out. I knew he would. He's taking her to a Fourth of July pool and picnic celebration at some rich friend's home out in the suburbs. She's a nervous wreck, of course. I went shopping with her and convinced her to buy an attractive two-piece bathing suit to replace her faded one-piece that looks like she may have had it since high school. So she'll look good, but I'm afraid she might need a few Valium to make it through this picnic. Or perhaps Michael could get her interested in grass by talking about the body chemistry involved in smoking. *That* might relax her. Jesus, I hope Michael can handle this situation—for both himself and for Evelyn. I convinced *him* to buy a new T-shirt because his others all have black-stained armpits. And he's been reading up on alchemy in the Middle Ages.

I've been so involved in this match this week that it made me wonder—do you worry about your patients like this, doctor? Or do you shut the door on them and forget them until the next time?

Of course, *you* can listen to anything. After all, it's only fifty minutes a day, even if it does become unpleasant. But what about the spouses who have to deal with your patients on a more realistic level? In other words (for I too am concerned mainly with my own particular drama, my own soap opera, even if I do switch channels now and then out of boredom or frustration or whatever), what about me sitting here tonight, the evening of our fourth wedding anniversary—alone. Jake has managed to be on duty again tonight. I could swear he *asks* the chief resident to schedule him on birthdays, holidays, anniversaries, any day that is important to me. And you know why? He's just damned afraid of his feelings. And afraid, apparently, of mine as well.

Four years. Four married years. Good God, what am I doing here? How did I deserve this? I don't even feel like going to visit the guys next door. Too fat; I just don't feel comfortable there any longer. Timothy is going to Europe for the summer—on some inheritance money, I think—so at least I won't have him staring at me and making nasty comments. I think I'm beginning to understand just how much vicarious pleasure I got listening to him make like Alexander the Great. More and more, lately, I have this unshakable fantasy . . . if I weren't pregnant, I'd seduce him . . . invite him in for a candlelight bath together . . . with a tray of wine and fancy hors d'oeuvres . . . back rubs and perfumed soap. . . . And then I have to feel so guilty just for thinking. . . . Damn it! Why isn't Jake home tonight? Perhaps he has someone better to spend it with at the hospital, some slim, shapely nurse or female medical student. You'd know before I would. He hasn't even called. I'm afraid to call him because it means having him paged, and then if he's actually busy with a patient I feel so ridiculous having called him—the neurotic, sentimental wife who needs reassurance.

How do women like me get themselves into this position? I mean, feeling so helpless even when they have proven themselves as bright, independent, productive women? Adam and I have talked a great deal about this, for it is a major part of my dissertation. I'm still trying to pull it all together, but the more I look into the biographies and the writings of my three subjects—Sylvia, Virginia, and Zelda—the more I suspect that it has something to do with their fathers, and their mothers' fathers before that, on and on backwards. All those remote or absent fathers—unresolved Oedipals? There's Sylvia Plath, whose father was twenty-one years older than her mother and who died when Sylvia was about seven, leaving his wife alone with his small daughter and a son. Sylvia chose to marry a teacher-writer like herself and wrote sunny, cheerful letters home to mother from her great English house in the country about her two lovely children and her husband. Until he started cheating on her. But her poetry has none of the Pollyanna sweetness of those letters; instead it chills one with images of Nazi boots and stark white hospital rooms and death. Her suicide (after two or three other widely separated attempts) should also, apparently, have been only an attempt.

Virginia Woolf's mother died when she was thirteen, leaving her, her sister Vanessa, and her two brothers, Adrian and Thoby, with their famous father, Leslie Stephen. Now, Virginia chose a supportive, apparently loving man for a husband—and yet we find she was not entirely comfortable or satisfied with that heterosexual arrangement, that she never had children, that she very much resented the "rest cures" imposed on her by her doctor and her husband, Leonard. Her books are beautiful, poetic, elegant combinations of words in search of their own harmony. What made this woman put rocks in her pockets and walk out to a watery death?

And then there's Zelda, not much of a writer, really, but her husband, Scott, accused her of stealing his material when she wrote, rather autobiographically, *Save Me the Waltz*. Zelda's father, a judge, had been a prominent public figure but a remote domestic one. What made this sparkling, dynamic, talented woman fall to waste, to the ravages of mental illness and painful eczemas and, finally, death in an institutional fire? How did all of these women fall into such dependency? What cursed psychological development causes even strong, independent, creative women to become such dependent creatures?

There are answers somewhere to all of this. Does the Freudian system have them? Can that Victorian, patriarchal mama's boy actually have understood the very peculiar position of women in our society? Well, back to my own drama. I've been writing to you through the late news and part of the late monster movie, which is just terrible. Good night.

Pleasant dreams,
JEANNE DANIELS

July 8

DEAR DR. FRICKMAN,

We had a Fourth of July barbeque this weekend for Sydney and Mandy. I posed as a striped circus tent in a new dress from Sears and played the role of perfect American hostess, offering three varieties of hamburgers, which I selected from a recent women's magazine (an impulsive purchase at the supermarket check-out). Listen to this feast. Besides a luscious fresh-fruit salad and two desserts (sour cream apple pie and carrot cake with cream cheese icing), we offered gourmet hamburgers: the Idaho burgers (topped with grilled green-pepper rings and three-bean salad); Pennsylvania burgers (brushed grilled burgers with soy sauce, topped with sauteed mushroom slices and diced pimiento); and California burgers (topped with thin avocado slices and sour cream and sprinkled with crumbled bacon). Now you may think this was all rather frivolous and a major waste of time and energy, even for the Fourth of July, but actually it turned out to be quite a learning experience, real food for thought, as I'll explain in a moment.

First, I want to tell you about Jake and Sydney and Mandy, who got into a long, heavy conversation about analysis, about Jake's analysis, while I played magic chef. Of course I deliberately stayed out of the conversation anyway (having learned that any burn I might receive from the grill would be far less traumatic than one resulting from such a conversation). After a couple of joints, everyone seemed extremely talkative, but I didn't expect them to get into such a serious conversation. Sydney and Mandy have known for some time that Jake is in analysis, but they've never asked any questions about it. They were dumbfounded to learn that he actually lies down on your couch and that he can't see you and simply says whatever comes into his head—and that he actually does that five days a week at seven in the morning—and that he pays you a reduced fee of thirty dollars per day for it all! Their startled looks and comments just made me chuckle; I had forgotten how strongly I had once felt about that. One grows accustomed to anything, it seems. But that was just the beginning. Both of them then started to compliment Jake, telling him that they really thought he was much more open, more friendly, less abusive toward me, more relaxed. And you know, I think they sincerely meant it. Oh, their brains were a bit loosened from smoking, perhaps, but Jake just basked in the sunshine of their glowing commentary. I must admit that I started to feel rather left out. All those changes—are they really taking place, I asked myself with new awe of you and the psychoanalytic process. Where have I been? I hadn't noticed any of it—hardly. As we made love that night to the rhythmic clatter and banging of our old air conditioner, I thought I detected a new tenderness, a greater sense of concern than before. . . .

But the next morning as I stood at the sink in eighty-eight-degree heat and 90 percent humidity (or maybe it was the reverse) scrubbing off the hibachi grill and washing glasses, I could only groan good-bye to your New-Made Man Miraculous, who had over-slept his tennis reservation and was rushing out the door to try to get a game in. So this is where the hamburger lesson comes in (this inspired insight hit me as I broke three wine glasses in the dishwater). All those varieties, all those different garnishes, all those pretty, decorative toppings, all those little changes—they all add up to one thing in the end: No matter what you put on top, around, under, no matter what changes in appearance, the product is still a hamburger—ground-up meat from a dead, dumb cow.

Luckily I was diverted from my labors, first by a telephone call from Evelyn and later by a visit from Michael. You will remember (in the continuing saga, Days of Their Lives) that they were to have their first "date" at a wingding of a picnic at some wealthy friend's parents' home. It was an all-day, almost all-night, affair with plenty of fancy food, liquor, and opportunities for recreation that included an Olympic-sized pool, several empty bedrooms, shuffleboard, and a private tennis court. From what I could gather from them, they had a terrific time and didn't play any shuffleboard. But each was worrying (each in a characteristic style) about what the other had thought of him/her. I didn't have to say anything. Both were obvi-ously starry-eyed. Michael didn't even complain about anything. Oh, I take that back. He *did* have his big toe bandaged in a rather ostentatious manner; stubbed it on the bottom of the swimming pool somehow or other. But outside of that I heard not a single complaint. Evelyn was ecstatic to find that Michael was so know-ledgeable about alchemy and chemistry, and she confided to me that she actually took off her beach robe and swam in her new two-piece and that Michael had complimented her while teaching her how to dive. She also showed great concern over Michael's big toe, so it looks like they may truly hit it off. I haven't received any physiological reports yet, only romanticized raptures. We'll see.

Much later in the afternoon, when I was busy revising the first two chapters of my dissertation, Nancy called. She only arrived home the day before from her month-long vacation with Brook in Italy. She was still recovering from jet lag but apparently eager to touch base with friends again. And, much to my surprise, she launched into a rather emotional outburst concerning how much she had missed her therapist and her group. God, how *dependent* you psychiatrists make your patients! It remains, even after all this time, a mystery to me. What in the world do you offer that holds people so strongly? Even a month in Italy, enjoying art treasures and beautiful Italian landscapes, antipasto and pasta, and exciting, passionate sex (for Nancy often mentions this topic, telling me how they always set aside time for making love in the afternoon or early in the evening instead of later when they might be too tired really to enjoy each other), even a lovely month away like that doesn't quite satisfy her like her therapist and her group. (Nancy sees him once a week and the group once a week.) I was *most* surprised, however, when Nancy asked me so much about Adam—how was he doing, did his wife go off to visit relatives out West as planned, had I seen him much lately, doesn't he seem like a cuddly teddy bear? Astounded, that's what I was, astounded. Or is it blind I am? I've definitely been awfully naïve. I'm beginning to think that you Freudians may be on one right track after all—about sex being such a pervasive issue, I mean. And so that makes me wonder about how sexually charged things must be in your offices. Is Nancy sexually attracted to that therapist of hers? Is Jake attracted in a similar way to you? I mean, Freud said, didn't he, that we are all bisexual to some extent? Well, it's just as well you don't answer my letters. I'm not sure I want to know about all this. Sometimes I wish I could just go live in Disneyland, such a pleasant, clean, wholesome place.

Greetings from
Adventureland,
JEANNE DANIELS

July 18

DEAR DR. FRICKMAN,

What in the world is the matter with Jake lately? He's certainly worse than ever. I imagine you will certainly have heard about it by the time you receive this. We had one of those money arguments again—the kind that leads to so much more that by the time we call a truce we're both saying, "Money doesn't matter." It's almost absurd to recount the actual argument; I think it started when I was talking—a bit manic, I admit—about saving for a crib I had seen down at Wanamaker's. (I went there after working in the library today and just looked around at baby furniture and nursery-rhyme lamps and lovely wooden cradles. And then I went to the infants' department and tried to be casual while looking around at tiny undershirts and gowns in pastel shades of blue and green and yellow and pink. And sweater sets with hats and booties that had ribbon ties on them. And warm, soft blankets with satin edges to pull up gently around a baby's cheeks. . . .) A crib—just a pretty white crib all brand new and beautiful—to lay our baby in. Jake acted like I was some kind of an extravagant, spoiled brat. I mean, is it so much to ask, a new crib for our first baby? Not gold-plated, not antique wicker, not even fancy colonial. Just a pleasant, unused bed for a tiny infant. Listen, don't think I'm wishing you ill or anything like that, but if you got sick for a week—the Hong Kong flu perhaps or a sprained neck or a gangrenous foot—then I'd have enough money to buy this lovely crib.

Ah, what's the use? There's no sense starting the whole argument over with you—such a blank anyway. But I want you to know once and for all that Jake is as constipated as ever in these money matters and that you are not one little bit of help—in fact, you are a great hindrance. Honest to pity, this is just not fair. Does he feel demasculinized because I'm making most of the money? Maybe he just really doesn't want a baby? Maybe not buying a new crib is his way of telling me he's changed his mind? Indecision is certainly another of his major traits, and you are also making that worse, from what I can see. How long have you been an analyst? I'm not really questioning your ability, Dr. Frickman, but don't you believe in speaking directly to him— ever? Why must he treat me like this?

As long as I'm in this mood (go ahead, say it, "bitchy mood," I don't care!), let me tell you directly what I think. If you ask me, his problem is womb envy or baby envy or creation envy, whatever you wish to call it. (This might even replace my Pursuit of the Giant Phallus theory.) It is my very definite opinion that you Freudians are much too hung up on the other side, that penis envy business. What could be more fantastic than becoming pregnant, watching not just a few inches of one's body change but watching and feeling one's entire body changing: larger breasts, growing belly, sensitivity to smells and tastes and, best of all, finally feeling that being move inside, a soft little feeling at first as it brushes up against the side of its warm enclosure, and then stronger and stronger strokes as the weeks go on, felt perhaps when one is quietly reading a book, or busily walking through the supermarket, or lying awake at 4:00 A.M., a kind of secret process that is going on so beautifully right inside one's body, that is being nourished by one's own body. An erection may be exciting, but how can it possibly compare to all that?

Again—what's the use? You'll manage to turn all this around. You always do. It will all still come out as penis envy in your mind. But heed my words; I just bet Jake wishes he could be pregnant. And maybe you do too—wish you could get pregnant, that is. Listening quietly each day to someone else's intimate problems, thoughts, and feelings is rather a womanly thing, don't you think? Do you know any men who actually do that outside of "business" (psychiatrists, bartenders, and maybe barbers)? Not many, I'll bet. But women—sure, there are plenty of women who listen all day, to their own children, to their husbands, to their friends, to strangers. Psychiatrists, maybe all doctors, are perhaps just frustrated mothers at heart—all "taking care." I suggest you explore all this a little.

We cannot go on with these senseless arguments.

Sincerely,
JEANNE DANIELS

July 25

DEAR DR. FRICKMAN,

Hello, doctor! The world is full of sunshine again. I'm flying high, feeling good about Jake, about me, even about *you!* This was just one of those weeks when everything seemed to come together to make me feel that our efforts have not been wasted, that the world may yet be a brighter place. Do I sound manic? Ah, perhaps so— but why not enjoy it while it lasts? Life is full of such ups and downs, and I'm ecstatic to be on an up for a change.

What, you might ask, has been happening that you haven't already heard from Jake? As you must know, he's not exactly the type to become enthusiastic, but surely you've noticed that he is in a better mood, has a brighter outlook, seems much less depressed? Several days ago he brought up the topic of internship and residency: Where shall he apply. After all, it's only one year away now, since he has officially begun his senior year this month. Where should this future great neurosurgeon take his internship—and where would we like to try out as a future home? *And* (I was almost knocked off my chair), where might *I* be able to land a college teaching position? Where do we want to raise our children (he actually used this plural)? What kind of a home would we eventually live in? Won't we have ourselves a lovely vegetable garden surrounded by flowers and lawns? And then we started reminiscing about our hitchhiking adventure the first summer after we were married; our six-weeks trip cross-country, sleeping by the roadside with our sleeping bags zipped together in our tiny pup tent, never knowing for sure where we would be next. The excitement of tornado warnings in Kansas, of bears at night in Yosemite—I loved it all: the greenness of Pennsylvania, the open landscapes of Ohio, the busy bigness of Chicago, the peaceful pine woods of the Black Hills of South Dakota, the unbelievably flat expanses of Kansas, a swim in a river in Missouri, the challenge of the hike in the Grand Canyon—and the lovely tired feeling we enjoyed over a charcoaled steak that night, and arriving at two in the morning on a beach in Orange County, California, our first view of the Pacific, only to have a huge tractor with a rake nearly kill us an hour later.

We had perhaps loved far-away, exotic California most of all, especially San Francisco. Why not go there to live? After all, we're completely free to choose. Or are we? Our talk, our plans, our reminiscences led us naturally into tender, wonderful, passionate lovemaking (big belly and all) until, afterwards, Jake brought up one little nagging reality. *You.* Can he, can we, leave you? Yes, I urge, yes, that's a whole year away yet, and he's already been seeing you for a year and a half. Surely by then . . . Silence. Obviously I'm an inteference if I urge such a move. It is an issue to be taken up with you. I'm the person truly involved, mind you, but he will discuss it with you. Well, I'm not worrying about it yet. I feel confident he'll decide to go—and leave you! We shall be a wonderful three thousand miles away if I have my way. (Ah, doctor, don't feel personally rejected. Think of it as if I'm your daughter and I have a healthy need to move away from you, my father, to make a psychological break, to have my husband to myself.)

My dissertation advisor (another father figure in my life— strange how all these father types keep popping up; it's kind of like carrying one's father with one no matter where one goes) approved my first two chapters with praise and encouragement. And—good news for me—he was terribly enthusiastic about an article I was inspired to write a few weeks ago about literary suicides, an investigation of how the methods of various suicides (or suicide attempts) reflect the metaphysical stance of the authors. It involved a comparison of Septimus Warren Smith (in Virginia Woolf's *Mrs. Dalloway*), who jumped out a window; Esther Green, who took too many pills and hid behind the furnace in Sylvia Plath's autobiographical novel, *The Bell Jar;* of the drowning death of Edna Pontellier in Kate Chopin's *The Awakening;* of the death by self-inflicted gunshot wounds in Katherine Ann Porter's "Noon Wine"; a slit throat in Ernest Hemingway's "Indian Camp"; of death by hanging in George Meredith's "Tale of Chloe"; and a few others besides. I wrote the article in a few days, absolutely an inspiration growing out of my dissertation. Anyway, Professor Ames thinks it is publishable, so I'm going to send it to some journal or another. I've been struck by the irony of being somewhat preoccupied with death just as life has become so precious—because of the life that is forming inside of me. What do you think that means?

One other event has contributed to my euphoria. Randy sent

me a beautiful letter. He has received some kind of award and a grant to write poetry and plans to spend a year and a half in London beginning in September. He included a poem in the letter, a finished version of a poem he had read to me in the Broad Street cafeteria back in April. It's about a solitary eagle, actually a metaphor for his mentor, whom we had discussed. He also sent me a book of science fiction inscribed, "For the rainbow of possibilities, for you," which I found a bit cryptic but somehow very endearing. What, what might my life have been like had I met and married a man like that—a sensitive, feeling, poetic type—instead of my rugged, macho, scientific, practical, adventuresome Jake? Ah—the rainbow of possibilities . . . and the choices one makes. Can we trust our collective unconscious to make the best choice for us? I'm just hoping now that you won't interfere in our right to choose where we shall move to. You wouldn't, would you?

As ever,
JEANNE

July 30

DEAR DR. FRICKMAN,

Jake began his six-week ob-gyn rotation today, and I couldn't help noticing that he still acted like a child being forced to go to his first day of school. He literally clings to me in bed in the morning; not because, as is more usual, he wants to make love, but because he doesn't want to get up and face something new, something unfamiliar. Of course he finally does, he always pushes himself, but this behavior occurs every time he changes rotations or begins anything new. Can it really be so difficult for him? Aren't you supposed to be helping him with a problem like this? Funny thing about it is that I used to welcome the clinging; it made me feel important, motherly, depended upon, loved. Now I only grow impatient with it. *I* want to cling to *him* and say, "Look at me, look at my body, which has grown so strange and heavy . . . just think that in just a few months we'll have a real live little baby to take care of, to be constantly aware of and responsible for. What will such an addition mean to our lives, to my life? Help me, hold me, help me handle this fast-moving change in my body, my mind, my feelings." But I don't say any such thing to him—he makes it obvious that he is dealing with quite enough at the moment. This is not fair, Dr. Frickman, this is not fair. How long, O Doctor, until my husband be delivered from these depths?

Am I being too dramatic? Perhaps. But dramatic is what I'd like, what I need just now. Once, *once* Jake came through in a very dramatic fashion, an act which probably led me to marry him. It was at the end of my senior year in college—almost a year after we had spent the summer together in the Catskills. There had been letters and phone calls and occasional visits during that year from his college to mine. I had decided that I loved him, but I suspected he was fucking around and wasn't really committed to our relationship, so I decided to go the following summer with my roommate, Genny, to waitress again in the Catskills. Without Jake. He begged me to join him at the Jersey shore, where it would be easy for us both to get jobs. As much as I wanted to, I said no, I had made my mind up. (And besides, a young man from my poetry workshop class named Jonathan Hurst, who was tall and had curly dark hair and sensitive dark eyes, had just been jilted by his girl back home, and he had held my hand in the library while we studied for exams, and we had sat together in deep mysterious silence on the great lawn by Old Main as the sun was setting, and I had trembled to be near him and walked on clouds when I was away from him. Such feelings made me think that I could survive without Jake—and that I might even be better off in the long run.)

But Jake graduated two weeks earlier than I did, and he called and begged me to join him at the shore. He already had a job at a kosher hotel on the boardwalk. I was in the midst of exams and in raptures over Jonathan Hurst, so I still said no. But Jake became dramatic, romantic, and I fell apart like a magnolia blossom in a high wind. He got on his motorcycle (only 100 cc. at the time) one night and rode it all the way out to see me—which is doing a lot, if you know what it's like to be on a small motorcycle that long on a cold night in early June. I was extremely impressed with this masculine display, enough to almost fail my Swift and Pope exam, enough even to forget Jonathan Hurst, enough to serve three meals a day to the luxury guests at the Sheraton Hotel on the boardwalk for the whole of that summer, and enough to marry Jake a year later.

So maybe it's time for a bit more drama. I'm afraid to be falling into these stereotyped roles. While we're students and childless, the the world still has endless possibilities. But Jake has only this one more year of school, and I'm writing my dissertation; I'll be a Ph.D. soon (if I can tear myself away from knitting booties and looking through catalogues at layette items and reading child-care books). What then will become of us? Maybe you'll turn Jake into a perfectly respectable, responsible, upstanding, conservative doctor who votes Republican. And maybe he won't want me to leave the children to go to work on my own and I'll be stuck with four kids and two cars and a bright yellow kitchen in suburbia. Why are you trying to change him? Maybe he should just stay as he is, after all. What if he becomes a different person from the man I married? Ah, I don't know, Dr. Frickman, some days I don't know which side of the fence I'm on. If I could just *know* what is happening. I feel like a little kid in a fenced-in backyard looking over the fence on tiptoe at two kids in the sandbox next door. Those two are having a glorious time for themselves constructing castles, demolishing bridges, deciding on their own rules. If I could only *see* clearly what is going on.

David has stopped working on my teeth for some time now, because of my pregnancy, so I don't get to talk to him very often. But he was here on Friday night to introduce his girl friend Pamela, who flew in from Colorado. While not a beautiful woman, her makeup, hair, and clothes all fit into the category of near-perfect, making her very attractive indeed. She was surprisingly friendly and seemed not even to notice David's bitingly cynical and sarcastic comments. I see he is still terribly ambivalent about having her here, and I know for a fact that the very young dental hygienist he's been sleeping with doesn't know about Pamela's arrival. Pamela and I quite hit it off on Friday night, so I wasn't surprised when she came over on her own on Saturday afternoon. She's puzzled by David's behavior, but only puzzled; not suspicious, not angry, not unhappy. I had to bite my tongue and just listen. Maybe that's why you say so little to your patients (or at least to Jake). I mean, if I said anything real to Pamela, she wouldn't hear it anyway—not after all the plans she's formulated around David. And is that what you think of me too? That even if you could talk to me, I wouldn't be able to listen? Perhaps, perhaps doctor. But there should be something, something to help me understand, so that I'm not left standing in my own yard trying to see into your sandbox.

Sincerely,
JEANNE DANIELS

August 10

DEAR DR. FRICKMAN,

Summer session is over. No more teaching. And we'll be going on vacation soon—camping in Arcadia National Park on Bar Harbor Island in Maine, as you probably already know. (And did you know that my ob-gyn said, "We don't let our gals go that far this late in their pregnancies"? I was set against going until *he* said that. "Our gals" indeed. What a world. Even having a baby is to be directed by a man.) Anyway, I all of a sudden have much more time to myself, to work on my dissertation, or, what seems to be more compelling these days, to fix up our hallway alcove, which has long been my study, as a room for the baby. I've already moved the desk out and painted the room yellow with white trim. And today I'll take up the rugs and see what I can do with the floor. Jake is showing mild interest in these proceedings; he offered to sand the floors if that's what I'd like, and asked about curtains. Actually, that's a lot of interest for Jake—even if I did have to push a little.

I'm going to miss teaching, I think; that feeling of having given a satisfactory performance, the sense of having touched other minds, of having excited people to go and read more on their own, the feeling of closeness with those students who are eager to listen, to contribute, to share their own lives with me. But I was starting to feel awkward (though rather proud too) about my ever-expanding belly. I had to be more—well, more ladylike; no more sitting down on the desk tops, much less walking around and waving my arms to make a point. Restrained, demure, not really me somehow. Obviously, my students have known for some time that I'm pregnant, but only two or three have said anything, even in our private conferences. But one woman (I'll call her Helen), a sophomore, came to conference a couple of weeks ago and with an embarrassed look finally blurted out the question she had come to ask: "Ms. Daniels, are you married? Uh, do you have an old man or——" I didn't understand her concern at the time and only found her question rather quaint, amusing. I assured her that I could put "Mrs." in front of my name quite legally, and that I did indeed have an "old man" at home ready to take up the responsibility of a child (although how much more there is to that statement I didn't even begin to explain). She did not bring up the subject again—until yesterday, when I had a phone call from her. Helen is pregnant, unmarried, and her "old man" has left the city, according to her. She's considering abortion, but she's scared, and she can't tell her parents, and what should she do? Tearfully this all came out. I'm not against abortion as a general rule; surely there are many situations in which it is better to prevent life. But as I sat there holding the phone and feeling this baby make strong, beautiful kicks against the inside of my womb, how could I reassure this woman that abortion was the best way for her? I tried, but the words stuck in my throat. So I sent her to Planned Parenthood. She needed a friend and I sent her to strangers. But I just couldn't—can't you understand? How many different ways one can look at a problem.

As I sit here writing to you I'm reminded of a dream, or part of a dream, I had last night. I found myself with two babies, one a girl, one a boy, and they both looked exactly like me, like my baby pictures, I mean. I only remember thinking in my dream, "These are two halves of me." That's all of it, all I remember. I mentioned the dream to Jake this morning and he just said, "You're not big enough to be growing twins." So much for insight and understanding.

Actually, I can't seem to get away from thinking about babies and children. Even in my dissertation. I've just finished the rough draft of my third chapter discussing Sylvia Plath's two children, Zelda Fitzgerald's one child, and the fact that Virginia Woolf as well as many other prominent women writers (Jane Austen, George

Eliot, Emily Dickinson, Charlotte Brontë) had no children. And then this morning I spent two hours in the student cafeteria with Nancy, who was upset by her therapy group because they confronted her problem concerning whether or not she'll ever have children if she decides to stay with Brook. (He definitely doesn't want to father any; he's much too attached to his life-style, his solitude, his travel, his pleasures.) So we got into another lengthy discussion of how women can have both a career and a family, and put up with a man as well. We sketched out the perfect man for such a situation: an equal partner, a man with a strong, sensitive "mothering" instinct (which I'm willing to change to "fathering" if it can mean the same thing—being sensitive to a child's needs), a man who can be supportive of his wife's career while building his own—such a man as I have not yet met, in short. If it weren't for the fact that all these studies show that a father is a necessary component of a child's healthy development, it would be tempting to do without him once he's done his initial "work" of fertilization. Anyway, Nancy says she *wants* a man too, even though her first marriage was a disaster, and right now Brook is that man.

So I'm getting to know what a lot of people think about having babies, children. Everyone but Jake, that is. He seems so reluctant to talk about what it's going to be like when we have one, what its name will be (what do you think of Barnett for a boy?), even what the process of birth will be like. He says it's "just not a reality" to him yet. I went to the hospital on Thursday night for a kind of orientation program to childbirth classes and for a tour of the facilities including the delivery room and newborn nursery. Prospective fathers were invited and encouraged to attend as well. Jake, however, had a dozen excuses (he's seen enough hospitals, he doesn't need to see a film of a birth when he's seen live births, his toe hurt, he had a lot of reading to catch up on, he'll make it to the next one, he has every faith in my capability, etc.), all of which added up to the usual "I can't deal with that" for whatever mysterious reason that can only be made known to you, no doubt.

Dr. Frickman, both of us, you and I, are going to have a problem on our hands if this doesn't become "a reality" in Jake's mind awfully soon. You know, even though you don't literally answer these letters, with pen and paper and written words, I do get the feeling that I'm being listened to, that we have a strange sort of cooperative effort going here, sometimes anyway. So look, I feel like I've been laying my cards out on the table and have been rather up front with you. True, I've been very angry at times, and I do apologize for my more heated expressions. Here's your chance to answer my criticisms about not caring about anyone but the patient. I'm trying to prepare myself for this child—and I do what I can to get Jake to think more about it—but my own feelings are just about all I can handle (and more than I can handle some days). So how about a little help? I mean, a little less denial of my obvious condition would help a great deal. Please?

Sincerely,
JEANNE DANIELS

August 14

DEAR DR. FRICKMAN,

Why is Jake so depressed again, still, yet? Why after all this time, all this money, all this talk, all this suffering? Is it me? Am I making too many demands? Am I too competitive, as he has accused me of being at times? Am I too competent, domineering, independent—or too incompetent, passive, dependent? Don't I bolster his ego enough? Do I expect too much of him? Am I overwhelming? Rejecting? Do I try too hard to please? Do I ignore his needs and pleasure? Should I cook better dinners? Plan better desserts? Initiate sex more often? Wear black lace and a garter belt? Play innocent in white silk? Stay at home more? Go out and find more of my own interests? Shall I talk more about my feelings about being pregnant and having a child? Pretend it's not really there? My patience, my ingenuity is played out. What, what does he want from me? I argued against this upcoming camping vacation for so long and finally gave in. Not enough. He wants me to be *excited* about it. OK. I went out and bought a new lantern, patched and aired our sleeping bags, planned meals and stocked up on canned goods, even bought him new fishing lures for ocean fishing.

But it's not enough, never enough. He still comes home barely recognizing my existence and runs out to play tennis whenever he can. My dissertation is nonexistent as far as he's concerned. And so am I . . . until we climb into bed.

It's your problem, doctor. I give it all to you. I cannot figure this out. Perhaps I'm just too close; perhaps I'm too much a part of the problem. Since I cannot really affect the situation, I find myself retreating. My friends, my family, my teaching, my books, all grow in relative importance as he remains fixated in analysis-land, which may as well be Peter Pan's Never-Neverland as far as I'm concerned. And I can hear the same refrain: "I'll never grow up, never grow up, never grow uuu-p! Not me!"

I guess I'm just not the psychiatrist I thought I was. I've even sent Evelyn to the psychological counseling center because I couldn't handle her sex hang-ups. (I'm not sure they did any better —sat her in a room listening to tapes on relaxation which were quite sexually explicit, and she was unable to turn down the volume.) But one of her fellow grad students in the history department has asked her out. He's divorced and has one child, whom he sees weekends. Evelyn is going to spend Sunday with this fellow and his kid at the park. I don't know where Michael stands in all of this; I've hardly seen him lately.

David comes over almost daily before Pamela gets home from work (she got a job at a bank downtown) and talks mostly trivia. He's not a person who really likes to talk about his problems or his inner feelings, but I know he's feeling upset, in turmoil over what to do about Pamela, who is living with them in that topsy-turvy, filthy apartment. She obviously expects marriage. David doesn't seem to be able to make a decision one way or another. All this is made more difficult for me since Pamela comes over and talks about how she feels. My first loyalties are somehow to David.

Any suggestions, doctor? I'm in the mood to sit back and let you be the expert. This is all getting too complicated for me. I want to sit quietly with my hands on my belly and rock gently in my brand-new secondhand rocker.

Sincerely,
JEANNE DANIELS

August 20

DEAR DR. FRICKMAN,

Why must you analysts all take your vacation in August? Because Sigmund Freud did, I suppose? That reminds me of an old saying of my mother's: "If Sigmund [or Nancy, or Donnie—a name to fit the circumstances] sticks his hand in the fire, does that mean you must do it too?" A lot of wisdom, that. Because of your ill-chosen vacation time and because of my husband's stubborn insistence, I am sitting at this moment in my sleeping bag, in a small Thermos Pop Tent, in Arcadia National Park, in Maine—against my ob-gyn's advice.

Jake is snoring beside me; it is 1:10 A.M. and I cannot sleep. I was uncomfortable lying down, I'm uncomfortable sitting up, too, with this huge belly resting on my legs as I write you this letter by the light of my flashlight. It is *cold,* might be in the low forties or even thirties. I am fully dressed in one of my sweet ruffles-and-lace maternity tops (to be pregnant is to regress to wearing clothing styled for a six-year-old) and my maternity jeans which, fitting so tightly now in my seventh month, might not make it another six or seven weeks. I also have two sweaters on and two pairs of heavy wool socks, and I have to go to the bathroom—out in the bushes. My God, no wonder I can't sleep! Actually, the baby is apparently wide-awake and, I imagine, getting me used to being awake at this hour too. He or she is moving around so much, it must be as cramped in there as I am in this miserable womb of a tent. What if it is so cramped that it decides to come out early? I can just see the park rangers calling an ambulance into the park from some backwoods town around here—and Jake asking me what all the fuss is about.

Well, I had better look for my shoes so I can go outside to piss. I'll be out there cursing you under my breath, depend on that.

I'm back and still shivering. While I was urinating out in the bushes, I thought of another aspect of this predicament. The fact is that I cannot put the full blame on you and your vacation time. I want you to know that I am aware of my own responsibility in this adventure—by giving in to Jake's persistence, I mean. But I'm not sure that even you could realize how truly and obnoxiously persistent and insistent he is in arguing with me. He is always ready to argue about *anything* with *anyone*—and he manages to make all of my objections (I'd be uncomfortable; what if I delivered early; my doctor strongly advises against it; I wouldn't enjoy myself; it is too much hard physical work for now) all sound absolutely groundless. His particular technique, which I'm *sure* he has learned from you, is to turn all my objections into questions (Why would you be more uncomfortable there than here? What would it matter if you deliver early? Don't you think I know as much as your doctor? Why wouldn't you enjoy yourself? What work is there to do?). He wears me down with his energy for arguing.

It wasn't until we got here two days ago that I realized just why we're here, hundreds of miles from home. He can't stand it. He refuses to treat me one little bit differently than he did eight months ago. I am to be as strong and as independent as ever, a "mother" who never changes. Which means that I am not allowed to be dependent on him, even in this round, puffy body that sometimes feels so foreign to me and quite frightens me. I have fears about the baby not being OK. I have fears about giving birth. I have fears about dying in childbirth (I've even had the fantasy that they would probably bury me in the dress I have hung conspicuously on the door, just cleaned, for Jake to bring me when I'm in the hospital so I can wear it home). He doesn't want to discuss any of that. He is too filled up with his own feelings about having this baby. So here I sit trying to warm myself up with the heat of the flashlight. It's after two o'clock now and I think I'm feeling sleepy and just a little warmer.

> Having a wonderful time,
> wish you were here (instead
> of me),
> JEANNE

August 25

Dear Dr. Frickman,

I knew that was you on the phone, as soon as I heard your few terse words: "Mr. Daniels in?" Mr. Daniels indeed. Did you think I was the upstairs maid or what? You knew it was me. You know that you knew—and that I knew that you knew that I knew. So why not leave a message? Or at least be courteous? I mean, you were hardly civil, so brusque and businesslike while I used the polite, modulated tones my mother taught me at the age of four. Don't you think I'm intelligent enough to take and give a message? Or do you think I'll play sabotage and "accidentally" give the wrong message to make Jake miss his holy analytic hour? Or what? I could scream; I wish I *had* screamed right into the phone, right into your sensitive well-attuned eardrum: Hey! I'm a person, too, Dr. Frickman. And after all this time I think I'm only now realizing that you are actually a person as well. You're not a bearded cartoon character out of the *New Yorker;* you have a voice, other patients, your own friends, a family, feelings, and thoughts, interests, and dislikes like everyone else. Well so do I. I exist too. And I'm married, for better or worse, to your patient. You cannot pretend that I don't exist! I can't believe I finally had an opportunity to talk with you and I missed it. But you just weren't about to allow any such infraction of The Rules, were you?

What did Jake tell you about the vacation? Do you know, he's really a different person on vacation, away from you, at least a good part of the time? Oh, he still has his silent, withdrawn times, like when he's fishing or running (one morning he ran five miles in the rain along the coast road), but on vacation he is somehow more together, friendlier, more relaxed than at any time home in the city, more like the man I fell in love with. We spent hours digging long-neck clams, and we bought live lobsters from the fishing pier and steamed them over our campfire. A couple who were camping next to us joined us for dinner—they were students from Boston—and added two wonderful bottles of wine, and we talked and laughed until quite late, like old friends. I could hardly believe how relaxed and friendly Jake was. After they left for their own tent, we sat together near the fire with a blanket over us, talking quietly and feeling the baby move. And I got him to talk a little bit about what it will be like. On the drive up to Maine, and on the way home, I read aloud to Jake—Malamud's *The Fixer,* which was lovely to share. And sometimes in the tent at night he'd ask me to read some poetry, which I was more than happy to do, trying to choose poems I thought he would enjoy. When he did fish (a project which bores me after a half hour) or run, I went into the town of Bar Harbor; one morning I had myself a solitary but most enjoyable breakfast of blueberry pancakes and hot coffee and cold orange juice, and then went browsing in the arty shops and book stores. I bought some lovely brown, glazed, pottery coffee mugs from a woman potter whose child played near her wheel in a small room in back of the shop, and I bought a beautiful blue and sea green batik scarf for my mother, and a hand-made leather belt for my father, a kind of gossamer white Indian cotton blouse for me to wear after the baby is born, a small, framed batik of sailboats for Jake (for his future office), and, last but not least, a tiny pair of soft leather moccasins for this baby who is already exerting itself to be recognized.

Actually Dr. Frickman, I seriously considered buying a gift for you as well—a small figure of a seal carved out of some kind of black rock; a little, silent seal, the kind that appears friendly but is apt to slip down easily into the dark depths of the sea, into a different element; an innocent-looking little creature who swallows a great many unsuspecting fish. But I knew it would be considered inappropriate, like a bribe. *Some* no-no, anyway. The taboos of analysis become more and more interesting.

Despite my feelings, now that I've had exclusive rights, so to speak, to Jake during this vacation, I feel that you and I are actually in a tug of war. The devil and the deep-blue sea you might say, hmm? Sometimes I just want all of this endless interpreting and analyzing to be over with. When I can get Jake away from it for a few days, I can feel again that we need each other, that we can depend on each other. I could swear he is more affectionate, more sensitive, more of a whole, real person when I have him to myself, away from you. This is not to say, however, that he ever fully forgets about you and analysis. One morning, for example, over our breakfast of slightly charred scrambled eggs and decidedly sour canned orange juice, he got me into the analyzing process:

JAKE: Do you think I'm more like my mother or my father?

ME: [Sensing danger of some sort] Hmm? I don't know.

JAKE: Well think about it, what do you think?

ME: Well, I hardly knew your father, I don't know.

JAKE: Come on, you knew him well enough. Do you think I'm like him? Or do you think I'm more like my mother?

ME: [Unwilling to be pulled into this] Oh, yes and no, I guess. I mean, a little of both. You have your father's penchant for hard work and your mother's dreams and ambitions.

JAKE: Oh yeah? What do you mean? What did you really think of my father?

ME: [Reluctant but warming] Well, you know I liked him. He was, well, he was an honest, kind, hardworking man. He was . . . he was your father.

JAKE: But you think he had no drive? No ambitions?

ME: Well, I didn't say that. I just . . .

JAKE: You said that he worked his fool head off while my mother sat with her empty dreams and pitiful ambitions.

ME: Oh come on! I didn't say anything like that!

JAKE: Well, then, tell me, tell me again. What exactly are you saying?

ME: Jake, what is all this about? What do you want me to say? I liked your father. I like your mother. So what are you getting so heated up about? Your father was a hard worker, right? He worked from dawn till dusk in the coal mines, and later he became a laborer and split his fingers till they bled and took orders from the boss. And your mother worked hard too, but she must also have had dreams for you to get beyond all that, to go to college, to become a doctor. Your father was critical, right? Like the time you had difficulty replacing the muffler on that old car. I got the picture: You were educated but you could never do anything right, had no common sense in his eyes. So I figure your mother and your grandmother must have been the real inspiration in your life. It was them who fed the fires of your ambition, who made you feel that you could do something with your life. Isn't that true?

JAKE: [Making himself more coffee, silent]

ME: Well? What do you think?

JAKE: About what?

ME: About all that I just said!

JAKE: [Getting out fishing-tackle box] Oh, I don't know. Listen, do you want to come down on the rocks and fish with me? Maybe we can catch our dinner.

Sincerely,
JEANNE DANIELS

September 3

DEAR DR. FRICKMAN,

Although I know it's in your records somewhere, and Jake may have reminded you in his free association, I thought I'd tell you, as a point of information, that tomorrow is Jake's birthday. He'll be twenty-seven. What adult-life development stage is there to look forward to at this age? Must be Erikson's "divided labor and a shared household," with a crisis coming over "generativity" and the development of the ability to "take care of." Now, let me get this straight: One has all of these phases, including some points of crisis, to get through from day one on up through seasoned maturity—until death, right? Now, from what I've been able to make out, if one has not been successful at one stage or phase, the next will be more difficult (if not impossible). Is that right? Well, where on this continuum is my husband? Is he going to be able to handle this new stage? Or am I likely to turn around and find him sucking his thumb and stroking a blanket? And me? Have I got it together enough (a phrase from my students, not my grammar texts) to meet this new stage? Sigh. "I get by with a little help from my friends . . ." You had better stick with us a while longer yet, Dr. Frickman. I have the feeling that Jake is having a terribly difficult time facing up to this coming event.

Hey! Want to know what I bought him for his birthday? Only you and he will probably ever know what he really thinks of it. (He usually accepts my gifts with a smile; no enthusiasm, no disappointment evident, no anything but a kind of polite smile.) As you must know, he has quite an extensive collection of model sailboats and pictures of sailboats—big, small, wooden, ceramic, stone, paper, old, new, elegant, sporty, some that can actually be sailed in a bathtub or lake or whatever—everything but the real thing, although the time is not now terribly far off when he may purchase his own and take that ultimate adventure, sailing around the world. For I do believe he intends to do that someday. Becoming a top neurosurgeon will not be enough for long. When he gets to that point (and I have every confidence in both his ability and ambition), he will be looking for yet another challenge and it will probably be the sea—that huge, watery womb. Anyway, back to his birthday present. I'd saved some money from teaching summer school and from my own birthday money to buy him an old, very intricately constructed schooner. It's only about eight inches long, but it is a handsomely carved and delicately rigged vessel, an antique I found while wandering around through old shops downtown. He will be able to pretend he lives inside of Hemingway's *The Old Man and the Sea* or in Conrad's *The Secret Sharer* or Melville's *Moby Dick* or whatever. Don't you think he'll just love it? I used to be angry with the whole collection, or, more truthfully, with the fantasy I think those boats represent. Just another escape from responsibility in the real world, I thought. Back to the womb to float around forever, or to the giant phallus setting itself up against death (all those terrible storms and sea monsters) in order to overcome that final challenge to one's own control over one's self. Either way I see it as representing a fantasy that does not include me; and after all, he did start his collection years before we were married. But maybe those are not his fantasies. Maybe he just likes sailboats. So I've decided to join in, to buy even more of these things, hoping to please him no matter what the fantasy may be.

Did Jake tell you that we went out with Evelyn and Michael

last Friday night? First to a Chinese restaurant in our little China-
town area, where Evelyn and Michael giggled over their fortune
cookies. Then we went to an excellent production of *The Taming of
the Shrew* down at the university. (When I see or read Shakespeare
I can't help thinking, who needs Freud? Or, perhaps a better alternative: Why not make Shakespeare required reading for psychiatrists in training? Why not suggest it at your next convention?) So
you see, they are together, after all. At least it looked good the other
night. Michael certainly looks happier, more animated than I've
seen him in a long time. And Evelyn glows, she truly glows. She also
went out with that history grad student who has a child—and liked
him, but what a heavy trip that would be. I'm glad I have these nine
months to get used to the idea of having my own baby. I can't
imagine taking on someone else's. I know that sounds terribly
selfish, but I'm trying to be honest; I think it would just be too much
for *me* to handle. Oh, but who knows what motherly instincts—if
there is such a thing—may grow in one? Sometimes I think I've
always felt like a mother.

Speaking of mothers, Timothy—who, I've decided, definitely
has some kind of mother problem (guilt at loving her when his
father died when Timothy was ten; feeling responsible for the
death; you know that scenario)—has returned from Europe. He
called and asked me to pick him up at the airport. His girl friends
must be out of town. And he must have forgotten how pregnant I'd
look. I knew what his reaction to me would be, but I went anyway
to pick him up. He was virtually shocked to see me sticking out so
far, and my chubby face and all. He didn't even recognize me at
first. He had a leather watchband for me, and he tried to be pleasant
as I drove him home, but he was angry. That's really the emotion
I think he felt. I understood, though, and was even able to feel
slightly amused instead of just hurt. (But it does hurt to lose his
friendship, if it can be called that, in some sense.) When I got back
to the apartment I made myself some lemonade, sat down on a living
room chair, put on some Brahms, and thought for a long time about
how people change and grow. Having this baby so warm and close
inside of me has made *me* change. I mean (can you, a man, understand this?), I feel so different now from how I did at the beginning
of the summer. I can almost say, "I'm ready." I hope I won't be so

dependent now on the approval of machos like Timothy. I don't need to reflect what they want. It's like Laetitia Dale in George Meredith's *The Egoist*. For years she makes herself into a mirror for Sir Willoughby Patterne (the egoist, also a male chauvinist) and realizes only many years and many hurts later that she has killed her real self, that she is empty. I won't do it. Not for Timothy, not for Jake, not for my father, not for you. You are, none of you, worth it.

Very sincerely,
JEANNE DANIELS

September 10

DEAR DR. FRICKMAN,

Everybody's going back to school. Everybody but me. What a strange feeling. I've been going "back to school" every fall for the last twenty-one years. Oh, I go to the library once a week or so, but I really don't have much research left; I just need to write this dissertation now; only three chapters to go, and I already have chapter four outlined. It's just getting to be too much effort to drive down to the university, look for a parking place, and walk (or do I actually waddle?) to the library. And anyway, I do, oddly enough, enjoy just sitting alone writing about these women authors, picturing them sitting alone with just pen and paper and their thoughts, like I do. I look out our bedroom window at the big sycamores that line our street. Their leaves are still green, pretending that the summer is not ending, that children are not once again passing beneath them on the sidewalk, shouting, laughing, dragging lunchboxes and books in sacks on their backs. Those broad green leaves pretending they will live forever, perhaps, or are they just enjoying those days while they last? They will be falling down, covering the sidewalks in crinkly yellow and brown when we bring our baby home from the hospital in another month or so.

Speaking of enjoying days while they last—I'm holding my breath at the pickup in Jake's mood and affect. When he began

this rotation in surgery he didn't even cling to me as I have
come to expect; he even seems happy in it now. Maybe the
choice of neurosurgery is a good one for him after all. I mean,
maybe he'll finally feel that he is at the top of the heap (the Cap-
ture of the Giant Phallus?) and that lifelong struggle will be
over; he'll be able to coast. At any rate, he is so enthusiastic
about surgery; it is truly exciting to him, isn't it? I can't quite
understand that, but I'm happy for him. He seems to have found
a mentor, too—that big-time surgeon, Henderson, who apparently has rather taken a liking to my Jake. Henderson should be
a big help getting Jake into the internship and residency of his
choice. (Does that make you jealous?)

His choice has been, as you must be quite aware, quite the topic
of discussion at our house lately. The issue came up again after I
talked with Adam and Nancy about applying for teaching jobs. If
we stay here, I can probably get part-time work teaching composition and introductory literature courses for part-time pay. But I feel
I'd be joining a big, anonymous pool of exploited workers, mostly
women. They call you when they need someone, that's all. I want
a real job, a real chance to show what I can do, a challenge, a place
to move from, upwards and onwards. With the job market the way
it is, I have to be willing to go where there is an opportunity—to
Oregon or Kansas or North Carolina or California or wherever.
The problem is, of course, that we must go where Jake has a good
opportunity . . . and then there is this baby to think about. When
will I be ready to go back to work? Anyway, I've been trying to
convince Jake that the best thing we can do for both of us is to
go somewhere else, to broaden our horizons. As I see it, you
are still the major stumbling block. Soooo—I have a campaign
planned . . . maps of California, pictures of San Francisco, flowers
in my hair. . . .

Adam and Nancy are both in the midst of applying all over
the United States for jobs, actually filling out applications, preparing résumés, writing letters. Adam can go anywhere (being a
man who will simply take his wife along wherever he can get a
job), but Nancy has a bit of a problem because of her emotional
commitment to Brook. I listened to them talk and talk about job
opportunities (and the lack of them) and started to feel very out

of place there in the student cafeteria with my huge belly. I got
this feeling of being somehow suddenly left behind. The night
after talking to them I dreamed that they got married to each
other (the divorce and separation which would be necessary for
such an event were not part of my dream) and went off to wonderful jobs somewhere—but they wouldn't tell me where. I
stood in my graduation gown and cried. Since having the dream
I've begun to think that my unconscious may have been perceiving some subtle vibrations between these two. Anyway, it was
just a dream. The point is, what *am* I going to do with diapers
and a dissertation? How does one merge the two?

Well, first things first. I have a campaign to wage. California,
here we come . . . or perhaps it should be, "California or bust."

Sincerely,
JEANNE

September 16

DEAR DR. FRICKMAN,

Did I ever tell you that Jake and I once *walked* across the
Golden Gate Bridge in San Francisco and that I pissed behind
one of the big pillars about halfway across only to learn that
they have closed-circuit TV camera surveillance on you all the
time—because they're watching for potential suicides? It was on
our hitchhiking trip; we got a ride over to Sausalito and walked
around the shops there for awhile, listened to amateur musicians
playing guitars in the park, and then hit upon the grand idea of
walking over the Golden Gate—something to tell our children
and grandchildren (and, it seems, my husband's analyst) about. It
had been a real high point (ha) in our trip—a kind of epiphany,
you might say—so I knew that bridge would be good ammuni-
tion for my campaign. Sure enough. All my books and broc-
hures and pamphlets and statistics (if nothing else, I have become an excellent researcher; I stopped at the travel agency after
the library) seemed to culminate in a picture of the Golden Gate

at sunset. Jake finally became as excited as I am about moving out there. Do not imagine that I have deluded myself into thinking the war (such as it is) is over. After all, he still sees you five times a week and he has to be accepted in a good surgery internship-residency program out there, and then I'm afraid old Dr. Henderson might be trying to convince Jake to stay on here under his tutelage. (This is a long shot, but you and Henderson aren't in cahoots, are you?) Jake needs to be on his own; *we* need to be on our own. I really can't tell from what Jake says if you're for this move or against it. I somehow expect the latter. If so, watch out, for I'm determined in this instance to take some control over my own fate.

Everyone will be moving away from here anyway—most of our friends, I mean. I'm sure Adam will get a top-notch job at Princeton or Yale or some place like that and Nancy may even opt for a good job instead of this semisecurity with Brook, and Michael and David and Timothy will graduate in June, and most of Jake's fellow students will be leaving the city. Speaking of going away, we went to a party at Nancy and Brook's this past weekend—something of a bon voyage party for Randy, who is leaving for London later this week. He'll spend a year and a half or more there writing poetry. At the party he played piano while a friend of his played a cello in a duet Randy composed. He looked up at me once as he played and I had to control a hysterical impulse to get up and hug him. Later, we had a chance to talk together for a few minutes. He was interested in my feelings about being pregnant, about having a child, about my academic work, and he made me feel beautiful (even if I do resemble a beach ball) and at the close of our conversation he solemnly handed me a flower, looked into my eyes, and just said, "I'm glad we connected." I smiled and floated home on my fantasies. Ah! I'm just so vulnerable in this condition. I love feeling this being stir within my womb, but I'm beginning to feel anxious about a return to reality or normality or whatever—my own separate, thin self once again. I really do think my perceptions, my feelings, are somewhat distorted by all these radical changes. Life will never be quite the same again.

But what about Jake? He's not pregnant. So can he understand all this? He seems so unaware and so uninterested. Here I was the other night at the party thinking he'd see right through me, realize how excited I was about Randy. I *was* half-afraid he'd read my mind or my feelings. It brought back to me my childhood idea that when I died I would have to sit through a movie of my life—every detail good and bad, every hidden moment, thought, and feeling to be revealed and repeated—the Great Movie in the Sky. But it's not like that. Nobody really cares that much about any one person. No one is that tuned in. Except! Except, of course, the great analyst. Perhaps there really *is* a Great Movie after all, only it's not in the sky; it's on the couch. One digs up every long-hidden thought and feeling, a whole life revealed in detail to be examined and interpreted. If one can direct and produce this movie with sufficient completeness and without falling apart, one enters the pearly gates of the Successfully Analyzed (whatever that means). If not, it's back to limbo, or worse I suspect, and one is buffeted around in the storms between id and superego. I must admit that it's a tempting, even intriguing idea, that one could talk out one's life in epic fashion and really gain perspective on the patterns within it. But no thanks. No Movie for me. I long ago gave up that absurd idea. No need to leave one's self so open, so exposed. No sir—I'm not going to be caught pissing on any more bridges.

Sincerely,
JEANNE

September 25

DEAR DR. FRICKMAN,

He promised. He promised to be home from tennis by 7:15 so we'd have time to pick up Sydney and Mandy and drive downtown to hear Van Cliburn play at 8:00. He didn't get home until ten minutes before eight; just strolled in and took a shower. Sydney and Mandy know this trick of his well, so they didn't even ask for an explanation—they could see the smoke coming out of my ears and nose—but I know they were terribly annoyed. Since they (or at least Mandy) often display their domestic problems, I didn't mind so much performing a short scene for them as we raced down Broad Street:

ME: Why, why must you always be late?

JAKE: We're not that late. What do you think you'll miss? These concerts always go on for hours.

ME: That is ridiculous, but it is also beside the point. The three of us have once again been inconvenienced by you. I hate to arrive late and have to disturb all those people.

JAKE: Jeanne, we'll only be a few minutes late. They never start on time.

ME: A few minutes? You'll drive all over for a parking place now, I suppose, instead of paying for the lot across from the theater? You just want to be late.

JAKE: And you always want to be early.

ME: Not early—just on time.

JAKE: [*Laughs*] On time. That shows how compulsive you are— and always trying to enforce the same kind of control on me.

ME: Oh, so that's it. You're taking this opportunity to constructively teach me that I'm too compulsive because I want to be on time!

JAKE: No, actually I think you fall more into the category of anxious. When someone is always early for everything it shows great anxiety.

ME: Oh, I see, on time makes me compulsive and early makes me anxious. What category, pray tell, do you fit into, always wanting to be late, always making us late for everything?

JAKE: [*Laughter*]

ME: Well?

SYDNEY: Yeah, what is it, Jake? I'm really becoming interested in this.

MANDY: Don't start, Syd. I was ready tonight, on time.

SYDNEY: Yeah, for you ten minutes late is on time.

JAKE: [*Malicious laughter*]

ME: Well, come on, aren't you going to tell us, O great teacher? What does it mean to always be late?

JAKE: Simple! Hostility. [*Still more laughter*]

SYDNEY: Christ, that's no secret! Hey, Jeanne, don't you think Jake and Mandy are two of the most hostile people we know?

ME: Jesus, Syd—we get enough of this at home. Let's change the subject.

But you know, Sydney is right. Somehow he and I, both people who wish to please whenever possible, have managed to hook up with our opposites, people who are indeed hostile, who seem to need always to be late. How do such things happen? Would life be terribly dull, I wonder, being married to a nice solid guy like Sydney? I mean, would we both be trying to please each other to the point of nausea? Maybe we both like to please but don't really want to have someone else treat us like that? Whatever happened to getting married and living happily ever after?

Anne Sexton published a sharp little volume of retold fairy tales, *Transformations*. The story of Cinderella ends like this:

> Cinderella and the prince
> lived, they say, happily ever after,
> like two dolls in a museum case
> never bothered by diapers or dust,
> never arguing over the timing of an egg,
> never telling the same story twice,
> never getting a middle-aged spread,
> their darling smiles pasted on for eternity.
> Regular Bobbsey Twins.
> That story.

This is reality, and most people are aware of it, it seems to me. You can find it in the funny papers, in cheap novels, in situation comedy on TV; "happily ever after" is, to say the least, a matter open to interpretation. So why do people keep doing it with stars in their eyes and expensive ritualized weddings?

Take David and Pamela. Of all the people I know, David is the most cynical and Pamela the most gullible. Now, would you believe that David is actually talking about marriage? He doesn't even have stars in his eyes. What he has is a couple of dental hygienists in his bed when Pamela is out and nasty words in his mouth when she's home. So why? Why marriage? Pamela is so trusting, so ignorant, so blissfully starry eyed. Must we fall back on the old formula that opposites attract?

Oh well. Back to this lateness-equals-hostility business. What are you going to do about that? I mean, it has taken twenty-one months (and I won't even bother calculating the expense) for you to interpret and for Jake to accept the reasons for his behavior—now how long will it take to *change* it?

Sincerely,
JEANNE

October 10

DEAR DR. FRICKMAN,

Jake is actually filling out applications for internship-residency programs in neurosurgery. I can picture him now, dressed all in surgical green cap, mask, and all, saving lives in dramatic operating-room scenes—what erotic feelings that picture calls up! No wonder I'm mad about Alan Alda on "M*A*S*H" (I'd jump into bed with him if he just looked at me). I mean, it's all drama; hardly ever do you hear about more mundane surgery like removing a kidney stone or a gall bladder or a varicose vein (ugh). Just blood and guts, life and death, after which any woman will fall impassioned into the exhausted (but not too exhausted) doctor's arms and bed. Enough, enough of this fantasy—I haven't been able to bear having sex these past few weeks; I'm just too huge, too uncomfortable. Why is it that these fantasies seem to come up more and more?

Back to applications. So! Jake has decided to put in his name at three hospitals in San Francisco and two here. I'm ecstatic, delighted, floating! We'll go. I know we'll go to San Francisco and we'll be rid of you and psychoanalysis (nothing personal, doctor) *forever,* unless Jake decides to have his analysis by phone. (No danger really, though; he is unable to talk longer than three minutes when it's long distance.) Not that you haven't done him some good, Dr. Frickman. *But so have I!* When he filled out applications for medical school four years ago, who do you think wrote three different versions of "Why I want to be a physician"? Me, the English major, of course. It takes a good deal of creativity and imagination to write such a composition, especially if they also want to know why you've chosen that particular medical school. Naturally—and I know you went through this a long time back—one cannot say, "Because I want a yacht and a yearly vacation in Europe or the tropic isles"; one cannot say, "Because being a doctor will give my ego total gratification, with all those nurses falling over each other to do my bidding and falling in love with me besides"; one cannot say, "Because I'd like to maintain a town house in the heart of the city and have a country or ocean-retreat home as well." One cannot even say, "Because I'd like to set my wife up in the best house in town with a full-time housekeeper and the best private schools for my kids, along with the best private swimming, riding, dance, pottery, and music lessons to make them well rounded by the age of eight." No, one has to find the correct balance of altruism and muted but honest avarice. One wishes to serve mankind, to meet the challenge of an exciting career, to stimulate one's own emotional development; and one also has a deep interest in research (thus not a threat to the doctors who evaluate applications). One has, of course, been interested in being a physician ever since the age of three (after pulling down Suzy's or Tommy's pants behind the hedges) when (if there was no father or uncle to imitate) one so admired one's own general practitioner, who still made house calls and cured one's measles and took out one's tonsils.

Anyway, whatever I wrote helped get Jake into medical school, the way I figure it. But this time, in these applications for internship-residency, he decided he would do it all on his own, only asking me to print neatly what he told me to write (after all, his writing is *truly* illegible). So he wrote it all, including the short autobiography several hospitals asked for. He handed it to me for editing and approval. As I say, doctor, he's come a long way. One problem, however, in his autobiography. His mother and father were there, as were his sister and his dedicated family physician and some of his professors (influential persons); and you, you were given a prominent place in the later portion. But me? Not even a mention, as if marriage and our relationship didn't even exist. When I gently pointed this out he quickly added two sentences. But the damage had been done. I do believe he's been working hard all this time with you not merely to become independent of me, but to get rid of me.

No. No, I don't really believe that. It's just that he needs to be rid of you; then he can acknowledge me again.

Because Jake's been so busy with these applications as well as his regular work, and because it's getting very close to my due date, my parents came down for the day on Saturday. My mother and I shopped downtown at Wanamaker's for a few more baby items to complete the layette. She was, as always, extremely generous and we came home with a great many little clothes and a beautiful pastel plaid blanket and a soft yellow bunting. I have everything neatly arranged in the drawers of an old bureau I painted white with yellow knobs. I love to take a break from my dissertation and go and open the drawers and just look at the little gowns and sweater sets and diapers and receiving blankets. My excitement is kind of difficult for me to understand; it's so different from what I think of as my other side —the part of me that gets excited about researching some obscure fact in a dusty library volume, the part of me that finds joy in bringing all the facts of my research together in a clean, concise paper on whatever pedantic topic. I have a hunch that the feelings beneath these two kinds of excitement somehow have a common source—something to do with creativity—but they are still so different. Do you understand this? I've tried talking to Adam about this, and although he tries to empathize, I'm not sure I've really made it clear to him. Only Randy, to whom I've been writing, seems to understand. When he talks about his music and his poetry and compares it to my pregnancy, I somehow feel a connection, that he has understood my feelings on some level. Well, I wish I could have coordinated these emotions or feelings or energies well enough to have finished my dissertation before the baby is born. But I've only just finished the fourth chapter, with two chapters to go. Funny, though, it doesn't seem as important anymore.

What do you think of "Jesse" for a boy?

Sincerely,
JEANNE

Part Three

‹‹‹‹‹‹‹‹‹‹‹‹‹‹‹‹›››››››››››››

October 14

DEAR DR. FRICKMAN,

It's a girl! A beautiful, perfect, eight-pound baby girl! By the time you receive this, that will no longer be news to you, I realize. But it is *my* news, after all. Right now this baby is all mine. Of course I am not claiming spontaneous generation or virgin birth or even mysterious paternity, but these nine months have been almost entirely my experience—right up to the labor room and delivery (as I will tell you in a moment). I scrubbed the bathtub and carried the laundry basket up two flights of stairs right up to the day before yesterday. And *not* because I'm trying to prove my strength. The furniture (such as it is) knows how I've asked for a bit of help. Your patient has denied this pregnancy whenever convenient.

But right now it is time for them to bring the babies—they ring a little bell and I am to wash my hands and cotton swab my breast (alas, hospital rules!) in preparation for cuddling this tiny person.

I'm back. You should just see her, Dr. Frickman. She does look a bit like Jake—the dimple in her chin—which, I must admit, pleases me for some reason. (Oh, what, *what* are these ties which bind so tenaciously?) Her little mouth is so soft and she has already caught on to sucking at the breast although my milk has not yet come in. When they bring her to me at the 2:00 A.M. feeding, it is even a more special feeling. The nurse turns on a little light over my bed (so as not to disturb the two bottle-baby mothers in my room who get to sleep through the night), and I have my own little warm, dimly lighted space—indeed like a cozy nest—in which to receive that miracle of a child all wrapped up in soft blankets. And even though she is now no longer inside and an actual part of me, we are joined again in that magic nighttime hour, isolated from all else, perceiving only each other.

Oh, I know. I know what you think, doctor. This baby is the penis I always wanted and couldn't have. I think that's a perfectly dumb idea—probably just a coverup for Freud's disgust with female functions. I mean, really, to envy the elastic tissue of a penis more than a real live *child* that one nurtures within one and then gives birth to in such dramatic fashion. . . . Well, anyway, today even *that* ridiculous notion cannot bother me. I have a child, my very own infant to hold and sing lullabies to, to laugh with, to cry with, to be proud of, to worry about—a child who is, as yet, unsullied by all of your analytical interpretations: a small being who will grow up, I hope, without wishing for a penis or, more exactly, without wishing for what a penis represents: all the privileges of the male in a male-oriented, patriarchal society, which, by the way, is a shameful, inhumane mess.

Before I close, I'd like to tell you a bit about labor and delivery. I've heard that most women are driven to recounting this experience and I fully admit myself to their ranks. But I'd also like to know *what the hell you think you are accomplishing with my husband and what the hell you are taking our money for!* Listen. As you know, we went to a few natural-childbirth classes at the hospital. Jake wasn't even willing to go to the last one—too busy. So I bought these Lamaze books and read them over carefully and practiced the breathing patterns on my own. I tried to get Jake interested, but he kept putting off looking at the books, just as he wouldn't talk about names either.

Well, he's nearly a doctor, I figured, and birth is not something new to him. He's going to be a famous surgeon, right? He knew what to do all right. He went to sleep on a chair in the labor room. Did he tell you about that? The nurses left me pretty much alone since my-husband-the-doctor was there with me. I woke him up a few times to tell him it hurt. He said, "You're doing fine, babe. Keep up your breathing." All I can say is you two sure have a long way to go. What a waste of money. I just stared at the clock in the labor room and composed this letter to you in my mind between contractions. Jake came to visit me for a few moments in the recovery room, after going to look at our daughter in the newborn nursery, and he seemed very pleased; but I couldn't help wondering if he was disappointed not to have a boy. I know he wouldn't admit it even if he was, so I didn't ask.

What is it going to be like at home now? I mean, you've somehow gotten him to the point of not expecting me always to mother him—taking and picking up his shirts, buying his sneakers, fixing his snacks, typing his letters—but must I expect some kind of regression again now that I have a real baby? I've read about such things.

Look, can't we cooperate a bit here, doctor? Can't you help him bring out or act out his better side—his healthier self—at least until we can all adjust to this new situation? Really, I've had it. I have been as supportive as I could be. Now I'm asking—no, demanding —some extra help from you. That is what we pay you for, dammit.

Jake says you don't say much. Start talking.

JEANNE DANIELS

October 26

DEAR DR. FRICKMAN,

It's 5:30 in the morning. I've been home a little over a week, and I haven't had more than four hours uninterrupted sleep in all that time. Now I know how brainwashing techniques work. I'd confess to anything if I could be guaranteed eight or ten hours of sleep. Fortunately, the tortures of this situation are more than balanced by the little rewards that are showered upon me at intervals. I've learned to be aware, even to look for any such rewards: the special, wonderful smell of this tiny creature, my daughter, the feel of her unbelievably soft skin against my breast, the surprising strength of her tiny mouth as she nurses, even at three in the morning. I sit in my rocking chair holding her closely, warmly nestled against my chest, and rock and sing after I've fed her and I want to cry with thinking what a very short time I'll be able to hold her like this. And yet I'm filled with pleasure when I see her doing *anything* new—a wave of an arm, a kick, a startled response when a fire engine goes by, any small random response that shows she is growing and learning. Ah, you see, I could go on for hours, but my time is so limited now. (As I write, I'm cuddling Bonnie against me with my left arm; she's gone back to sleep, and so shall I!)

Now it's 10:30 in the morning. Jake has left for school; my mother, who was here for a week, has gone home. So it's just me and Bonnie, on our own, and I confess to being a bit frightened. She went back to sleep this morning around 5:30 and woke again at 8:30 to nurse and stayed awake for just a little while. I'm sitting here now with my first cup of coffee, determined to write just a bit more to you. I want to tell you what it has been like, from my viewpoint, to have made this addition and to have become a real family. The day Jake brought me home (two days after delivery) was a long one indeed. Although I felt fine, I didn't much appreciate his stopping first at the bank and then at the food store; my breasts swelled with milk and my stitches became increasingly uncomfortable as I sat waiting in the car. At home, we laid Bonnie in our one family heirloom, a white wicker bassinet that had been used for me and my brother and many cousins, and my brother's child as well. In the afternoon, we experienced our first bout with fussiness. I had fed her and changed her and made her warm, but not too warm, and burped and rocked her and fed her some more. But still she cried if I laid her down. After three hours of this, I was exhausted and insecure and felt like a child myself, longing with all my being for my own mommy (who, thank heaven, was coming the following day). Jake tried holding Bonnie when I begged him to relieve me for awhile, but as soon as she started crying, he'd hand her back to me. At around 8:00 P.M. she finally went back to sleep, after I had once again nursed her and wrapped her snugly in a blanket. Then Jake, who had been sitting all afternoon at the dining room table reading his medical books, put on the stereo and took her from me. The music of "Greensleeves" came on the radio and we just sat together looking at our sleeping miracle, and Jake's eyes filled with tears that overflowed onto his cheeks. I'll never forget that moment as long as I live.

Nancy and some other women from my book group and from

school have already been to visit. My mother was wonderful about making sandwiches and tea or coffee or whatever for all visitors. And every day new gifts arrive in the mail. I was especially touched by a gift from Dr. Moser and his wife (Dr. Moser is on my dissertation committee), a beautiful pink and white checked quilt and pillow which I'm sure Mrs. Moser picked out. I've never met her but heard much about her—she is a lawyer and a feminist and has recently undergone radical surgery for breast cancer. I felt, somehow, that here was a woman who could really understand the conflict I feel about—well, about having both a brain and a body is the only way I can express it right now. I mean, she probably knows, from her husband, about my career as a graduate student, my fellowship, my interest in feminism, whatever. And here she is, reaching out of her own troubled life in this generous and meaningful way to approve of me. Does that sound silly? Perhaps *approve* is not the right word, but I do feel that she has touched me in some unspoken but important way, that she has shown her support from woman to woman, sister to sister.

I can't write any longer. I'm full of coffee and yet falling asleep even as I write.

Thank you, doctor, for your congratulations, which Jake dutifully conveyed to me.

Sincerely,
JEANNE

October 31

DEAR DR. FRICKMAN,

I would not have believed, even a month ago, that I could have become so absolutely preoccupied with a baby, with my Bonnie. I read not at all—except perhaps to skim short journal articles when I go through the mail; and of course, Dr. Spock; I write nothing—except for these letters which I've come to view as a necessary outlet, similar to but different from my journal. Oh, yes, I've also been writing a lot about Bonnie in my journal, kind of preserving all of these wonderful and sometimes anxious moments on paper. The realities of my day seem to merge with my night dreams. I mean, I can think I've gotten up out of bed to nurse her only to waken and find myself and the sheets soaked with milk because she has slept a bit longer than usual. And I got back the pictures we took the first week I was home, pictures of Bonnie asleep in her bassinet, a picture of me nursing her, one of my mother changing her, a picture of my father smiling down at her in his arms. Since getting those pictures I've dreamed again and again of my smiling self joyfully handing Bonnie over either to my father or to Jake. In the dream they always smile back. But in reality, when I ask Jake to hold Bonnie, he acts as if I'm forcing some very foreign role on him, and the second she fusses he insists she wants me. Why is that, Dr. Frickman? You know, sometimes I do feel really desperate for an answer from you. . . .

Michael and Evelyn came together to visit and see the baby. They brought two little stuffed dolls, Raggedy Ann and Andy, which I've hung on the wall near Bonnie's changing table. They (Michael and Evelyn) hold hands and coo to each other as if no one else was around. It amazes me to see them like this, and they quite fussed over the baby. Good sign for Evelyn. If you believe in happily ever after.

Bonnie will be awake soon. I guess you'll just have to get used to shorter letters. Sorry about that.

JEANNE

November 10

DEAR DR. FRICKMAN,

Will you take a recommendation from me, a literary and humanitarian suggestion? The book group met at my house last night; we read a collection of short stories which, I think, has affected me more deeply than anything I have read in my career as a literature major, and perhaps more than anything I've ever read. It was Tillie

Olsen's *Tell Me a Riddle,* more specifically, the story by the same name. I cried aloud reading it; I could hardly see the words through the last ten pages. It is a woman's story, a mother's story, a human story. I urge you to read it. The author, Tillie Olsen, is in her sixties, the mother of four children. That impresses me almost as much as the book. No wonder it is so special, no wonder it touches chords untouched before. Here is a woman writing about a woman's experience in a most honest, most profound manner. I can't tell you about it; you must read it.

As we talked about it in book group—and for once we all agreed about a book—Nancy was holding my little Bonnie, cooing to her, cuddling her. I felt at that moment (I'm not sure I can express this without sounding sentimental) a bond not only with Nancy and the small group of women in my living room (some of whom have adolescent children, some of whom have been on the pill for five years, and some who are childless) but indeed with all women. I'm not saying, I hope, that anatomy is destiny or that children are the only and complete fulfillment for a woman, but that a woman's ability to nurture a child, to be an integral part of the natural creative force, sets her apart from the other half of the human race. I do not deny you the importance of the mighty phallus, of the deposit of sperm, but how it shrinks in comparison with the process of gestation, birth, and the growth of a child. I felt that Bonnie, my wonderful, beautiful daughter, belonged there, one of us, the women of the world who must look after, who must take care, who must preserve the continuity of human existence. I'm trying to convince Jake to read *Tell Me a Riddle,* or perhaps I'll read it to him on our next vacation. I've already sent off a copy to Randy in London.

Listen! Another breakthrough for Jake. Maybe, just maybe, you do help sometimes. He came home two days ago and announced that he was going to give Bonnie her bath. Never mind that I had given her one in the morning; why even mention it? Of course she'd love a bath, I assured him. And he was wonderful! He cradled her closely in his arms and held her with great care in the little tub of water I prepared on the kitchen counter. And he insisted on powdering, diapering, and dressing her himself. I think it's terrific that he thinks undershirts are unnecessary, and I laughed with joy when he discovered for himself that she really does smile, that it's not "just gas" as people seem to think in these early weeks! You know, I have so much enjoyed the pleasures of nursing and holding and comforting; even—or especially—the night and early-morning hours, when I sit in semidarkness having just changed Bonnie, and hold her close to nurse her. I rock in the chair, half-asleep sometimes, and dream about Bonnie's future, or think about my own immediate existence, about my dissertation, about Jake and his very different world. How I cherish the privacy of those moments. And yet, how beautiful it is to share that kind of wonder and joy with Jake when he does something like this—giving Bonnie a bath, I mean. But still, and I hate to complain after all this positive feeling, why must this kind of thing be such an occasion? Why can't Jake do a good deal more of this primary-care kind of thing? It's not simply that I want physical relief from such tasks, but I need him to share the psychological burden of it all, to feel that he is also responsible for the well-being of our child. Do I ask too much? Did holy Freud advocate strict separation of chores and responsibilities according to sex?

Sincerely,
JEANNE DANIELS

November 19

DEAR DR. FRICKMAN,

Jake is a wreck, a physical, mental, and emotional wreck, because of this demanding rotation on emergency-room care (a rotation which he *elected* to take, I might point out). He's probably mentioned to you some of the cases he's encountered—the motorcycle-accident victims, one of whom died after twelve hours in intensive care; the twelve-year-old overdose victim who had her stomach pumped out, regained consciousness, and then screamed and cursed at Jake for having brought her back; the chronic drunks, men who should be our revered elders but instead are the pitiful garbage of society, whom the policemen merely drag into the emergency room; the frightened young woman in labor who had not seen a doctor or received any kind of prenatal care; the hysterically sobbing man who has just heard his wife pronounced dead-on-arrival of a heart attack. The problems, the hours (including on-call duty every fourth night), the duties are all physically demanding and emotionally draining. I admit that much, and I sympathize to a point. But (ah yes, here goes the bitch again), but when Jake arrives home he is so full of his suffering in the service of mankind that he is unable to see me as a person who is also physically and emotionally drained by the twenty-four-hour, always-on-call schedule here at home. Not to mention the intellectual frustration when I think about my stacks of note cards and research waiting to be written up into a dissertation. He is no sooner in the door, even after having been away for two days and a night, than he is announcing that he *needs* to go play tennis. If I object, I am such a bitch. He reminds me in self-righteous tones that after all, he hasn't been out drinking with the boys or having rendezvous with women of the night; he has been in the ER mopping up the dregs of humanity (and you *know* if there was any mopup it was the nurses, almost all female, who did it). How dare I object to his going out for a little relaxation? And why not simply serve supper later?

At least—and I can't help coming back to this point again—at least he has you to talk to for a full fifty minutes a day. He can let off steam and complain to you about the sufferings and hardships of his life—including me, I suppose. But I am here in this roach- and mouse-infested apartment *every day* (I pack up Bonnie and all the necessary paraphernalia when I can think of some place to go, but I have no friends with babies, no family close enough to visit), with practically no one to talk to.

Well, that's not quite true. There are visitors at times. But they are mostly filled with their own problems anyway. Like Evelyn. She came the other day and brought a friend, another history graduate student named Sara, whom I've met before; Sara's husband is already a doctor, an internist I think, who's been in private practice for a year or two. Well, I spent four hours talking to the two of them —bathing, changing, nursing Bonnie all the while until she went to sleep—about their problems. Sara has recently suffered through her third miscarriage with, apparently, very little sympathy, attention, or affection from her doctor-husband. So she has made her mind up to leave him, at long last. But she is angry, angrier than I have ever seen anyone, I think—angry that she helped him through medical school, angry that he has not been able to communicate with her at times of deepest crisis; so angry that she talks even about suicide with angry threats. All this from a person I hardly know. But her anger touched me, made my own corners of anger flare up in defiance and desperation at a society that is too much directed by men, so I ended up promising to help move her out of her house (she swears she wants very little, and wants to only take her own personal things, like clothes and books) sometime next week. We can pack her stuff into my car; she's moving in with friends downtown.

It wasn't only Sara's problems we discussed during those four hours. Evelyn needs to split too; not from a husband, but from her father, who is a semi-invalid and who depends on her to care for the house. She's twenty-six and needs to get out on her own. Her sister and brother have long since left and started families. No doubt about it, she suffers in that situation; I say this even though I've never heard her complain about it before. But she is uncomfortable having anyone visit at her father's home. I guess Michael has been urging her to move out too, even suggesting she move in with him (*and* the guys *and* Pamela) next door to me. She has, wisely I think, rejected that suggestion. I'm going to help her look for a place she can afford.

When they left (it was a night Jake was on overnight at the ER) I was struck by the similarity of their situations—one escaping from a husband, the other from a father. Situations of tyranny. Or will you call this mere projection, Dr. Frickman? Ah, perhaps, perhaps. But I do seem to find plenty of confirmation of my own feelings in the real world, in talking to other women. Why do women seem to be less in control of their lives than men—or is that too a gross misperception? Is it a problem of humanity, generally? Isn't control of one's life the carrot that is held out to those in analysis? It *should* be the right of every man, every woman, perhaps every child.

Enough! I must sleep, and sleep perchance to dream of what alternatives there are. . . .

JEANNE

November 28

DEAR DR. FRICKMAN,

Jake came home tonight and collapsed on the couch, didn't even mention dinner, so you know he must have been dead tired. And Bonnie has finally gone to sleep after an extremely fretful day; she has had diaper rash, which bothered her (and therefore me) for two days. Apparently, the ointment I was using to clear up a mild rash just irritated it into a more serious inflammation. Having settled that problem (which took nearly all day) with the pediatrician on the phone, I switched her over to a medicated powder, and it seems we're all set here.

So, I now have some time to myself, with no responsibilities to anyone, for a few hours at least. Jake's white jacket is clean; Bonnie's nighties and diapers are all laundered and neatly folded in her drawers. It's 10:30 P.M. and I've decided to get out my dissertation materials and get to work.

Adam came over for lunch and to see the baby the day after Thanksgiving. It's the first I've seen him since Bonnie was born, and it made me realize how much I miss some intellectual conversation. He has finished his dissertation and is having it typed—by his wife. I turned green with jealousy, especially when he also started telling me, again, about where he has applied for teaching jobs.

What did Jake tell you about Thanksgiving? We stayed overnight at his mother's, but his sister prepared Thanksgiving dinner. We got into a conversation about our moving perhaps as far as California. The idea did not go over well. I think they—his mother, sister, uncle, and aunt—rather expected him to come back to their small town and set up a general practice, perhaps make house calls. I felt a little guilty; maybe he'd like best to be there close to mama after all and I'm keeping him from it. It's that kind of place where people do come back, do stay near their parents for life. So the talk of moving was quite a shock. But even more of a shocker was Jake's insistence on getting Bonnie and me up at 4:30 A.M. to drive back to the city so he could meet with you at 7:00 A.M. His mother couldn't believe it. He tried explaining that he'd have to pay you the thirty dollars anyway if he missed—and that brought up another subject, the astronomical cost of this "low fee" analysis. Jake's father was a laborer. During most of his life he probably made, in a long work-week, what Jake spends on five hours of analysis in one week. To his mother—and indeed to me at times—that is incomprehensible. To look at it through her eyes made it fresh to me once again, the absurdity, the elitism of it, I mean.

Oh! Just some news to keep you up on things around here. David and Pamela got married over Thanksgiving break. They went up to his parents' home in Rhode Island, didn't ask *any* of us to the wedding. Isn't that strange? Ah, another chance for happily-ever-after.

Must get busy on my dissertation. I will finish it in time to receive my degree in June. I will, I will, I will.

Sincerely,
JEANNE DANIELS

December 1

DEAR DR. FRICKMAN,

Now I know who you are! I found out this past weekend. I *really know now who you are.* Since neither God, Allah, nor Yahweh have a real place in your system, it must be that you are Freud reincarnated, beloved, respected, feared, hated, and adored!

I had thought to have a pleasant little dinner party with the two other medical students that Jake is in service with at the hospital's emergency room. I thought they might enjoy a relaxing evening away from all they have to put up with there. Only after the evening was half-over did I discover what a treasure they were—I'm speaking of *your patients,* Jan Hopkins and Russ Marsh. We discussed—or rather, *they* discussed as *I* listened—only *you* for the rest of the evening. They couldn't seem to leave you out of any topic that came up. They all seemed fascinated to be together, like a long-lost family, three children talking about Big Daddy. I won't say they all *agreed* about you; one participant, in fact, seemed quite hostile. I heard about how you fell asleep *twice* during analytic sessions and how this person had been tempted to pour cold water in your hand to make you piss in your pants! Ha! Wow, I learned more from those two about you and analysis in two hours than I learned in two years from Jake! (Was I ever tempted to add my two-cents worth of information about you. I could almost hear myself saying, "And he never answers letters!" I decided it was inappropriate, however.) Delightful, delightful. I must admit, I quite feel like I've been spying on you in your bedroom—an analytic voyeur, viewing the primal scene. What effect do you think it might have on me, doctor?

To tell you the truth, the evening was, for me, a combination of masochism (poor me, no analytic daddy to talk to or about) and amusement, especially about the very apparent sibling rivalry. The three of them were so curious to know about when each had begun analysis (sort of establishing their ordinal position) and about how each *felt* about you. Actually, I guess they were trying to determine (as indeed I was) how you feel about each of them. If they act as childish in their analytic hour every day, I do not envy you sitting there listening. I guess this regressive behavior is inevitable and even helpful to the psychoanalytic process, but I'd sure rather spend my time with Bonnie, who is at least cute and affectionate! Obviously, you are neither!

As ever,
Jeanne

December 14

Dear Dr. Frickman,

So what is this sudden turnabout on sexual desire? What has happened to Don Juan? I mean, is it that he's so tired working in the emergency room and all? Does he have a willing night nurse? Is he becoming impotent? Does he find me, now a mother, undesirable? He was so eager after Bonnie was born; we had long conversations in which he convinced me that the six weeks rule was absurd, that once the episiotomy was healed there could be nothing to stop us (or him). But now all of a sudden, after I've gone and had an IUD put in, he's turned cold, tired, unresponsive. I must admit that I am floored. He won't talk to me about it, just says he's tired, and only occasionally when I really coax will he turn on and become something of his former self. Wow. Talk about the tables being turned.

You know, I really hate writing about this to you, but then there's no one else for me to talk to about it, is there? Not Evelyn, God no, I just got her settled in her own apartment in graduate-student housing (some chronic upper-respiratory disease conveniently hit the former occupant, who had to move back home mid-semester). Not Sara, whom Bonnie and I also helped move amidst tears and death wishes (toward her husband) and random thoughts of suicide. Not Adam, my sometime-psychiatrist-philosopher-poet; we've grown apart since I've become a mother, or perhaps since I became pregnant. There's Nancy, whose been through a marriage, a divorce, and a passionate affair or two, but she's so *un*repressed, *un*inhibited I'm not sure she'd understand my situation at all. Not cynical David or innocent Pamela; they'll have enough of their own problems to work out. Not Michael, who is deep into solving his own sexual problems. Not Timothy (and this hurts because we used to talk so much about the details of *his* life), not Timothy, because he treats me like I have the plague. No, more accurately, he seems to have written me off as a dishpan, dishrag housewife and mother, dull, boring, unworthy of the merest attention. Oh, even more than that; he seems even rather contemptuous of me as a mother. Sigh. How that man must hate women.

I'm actually in tears thinking of all this—but I can't dwell on it. I have a lot of Christmas shopping to do yet, and Bonnie needs my smiles, and Jake must need some special attention, and I'm working again on my dissertation. As much as I need someone to understand me, I cannot afford to sink into one of the soul-searching analyses that you lead your patients into.

I just went downstairs for the mail. One bit of brightness which improves my mood a great deal—a long, newsy letter from Randy in London. He apparently thoroughly enjoyed the book I sent, *Tell Me a Riddle* (did you read it yet, doctor?), and he's doing a good deal of writing and even a little composing. He may teach a poetry course at Oxford next semester. He is filled with the sense of his own creativity, with pondering the mysteries in the depths of his own soul, with the wonder of his own destiny. As I read his thoughtful, enthusiastic words I feel myself stepping out of my self to become two people, one who sits here involved in husband, baby, friends, and another who is quite alone, free to travel, to have long periods of time all to herself to write or to read or simply to think. Even as I write this I realize it's not going to sound good to a psychiatrist, but, you know, I sometimes do really wish I could be two people—have two homes, two separate wardrobes, two entirely different life-styles, the best of both worlds, so to speak. Can you understand this? I'd be willing to bet there are many women who feel this way, who don't want to give up being mothers or even wives, but who would like to have the freedom to be active in the outside world, to forget shopping lists and detergents and baby schedules and immerse themselves in more intellectual or cultural studies. Oh, don't tell me that the majority of men are not out there in stimulating pusuit of intellectual and cultural peaks; I know that. But those who are do not have to deal with the conflict I am feeling. Oh, what's the use. You'll reduce all this to penis envy again, right? Most of the books do. There must be a way to solve this problem without resorting to sulking, schizophrenia, or suicide. But I don't know the answer; do you?

JEANNE

December 19

DEAR DR. FRICKMAN,

It's beginning to look a lot like Christmas . . . everywhere you gooooo. . . . I feel like a kid again, such anticipation and excitement. I've been busy shopping and doing a bit of decorating—some pine boughs and candles and ribbons for Christmas cards—so I've been into the spirit for awhile already. But Jake, who has been so involved in the hospital, just finally caught it this weekend when we picked out our tree on Friday evening and decorated it on Saturday with the help of Michael and Evelyn. Michael had never decorated a tree before, so we went all out with popcorn and cranberry strings, besides all the other little figures and balls we've accumulated in the past few years. Even though we won't be here for Christmas, we decided we had to put up a tree, not only for our pleasure but also for the added satisfaction of firmly establishing our own traditions and customs. My family always has had a huge family reunion on Christmas Eve, which we'll go to, but we want something of our own as well. On Christmas day we'll travel to Jake's mother's home and have Christmas dinner with his relatives. Both Jake and I are especially excited at showing off our little girl this year. I bought her an adorable soft yellow knit outfit; she's absolutely the most beautiful . . . Oh well, if you have children you must know all I'm about to say! Oh—and surprise of surprises, Jake brought home a little red flannel nightgown with a matching tas- seled hat for Bonnie to wear. He actually went to a store and bought it himself. (Believe me, that's a big step.)

Becoming parents has made both of us, I think, feel more like adults, no longer the uncommitted, isolated, idealistic, carefree (well, that's not quite true, is it?) students of our past. On Sunday we helped both Evelyn and Michael move Michael's things into Evelyn's apartment (this was a surprise to me, as it may be to you, but I'm very happy about it), and later we talked about how we felt kind of, well, kind of old—like old married people helping out some kids. I think I can really see Jake growing up. How much *you* have to do with this, I can't say, but I think it might make our lives a lot easier (no false hopes!). I'm reminded of the biblical line that goes something like, "When I became a man I put away childish things." That's what it's about.

A concrete symbol of this new sense of responsibility is Jake's new reluctance to use the motorcycle—especially since seeing the results of that terrible accident. On the other hand, when an insur- ance salesman called recently to try to sell us insurance, Jake star- tled him (and me) by saying not only that he could not afford it right now (true), but that he didn't see any immediate need. The gray- suited salesman, who looked somehow very out of place sitting on our Indian-print-covered, used sofa, patiently smiled and politely inquired about what would happen to "your beautiful wife" and "new little one" if something were to happen ("God forbid") to Jake. Jake smiled right back from his position on the cracked-vinyl chair on the other side of the telephone-spool table and told the salesman that he truly thought we'd be better off without him. The man left soon after, without even finishing his cup of Maxim. I don't expect him to call again. Which just goes to show, I suppose, that one must expect regressions as well as progressions. Right, doctor? But the hostility *is* a bit unnerving. . . .

And where will *you* be spending the holidays?

Enjoy,
JEANNE DANIELS

December 28

DEAR DR. FRICKMAN,

Merry Christmas! (Or Happy Hanukkah—I haven't been able to find out even that much about you. Season's best greetings, at any rate.) I am in the mood to feel quite benevolent—even toward *you* today—or even especially toward you. We're at my parents' home again, for the holidays. The change in Jake is unbelievable. I guess I've been realizing this gradually over the past few months, but here with relatives I have been able to observe how differently Jake is relating to other people.

I'm not sure I can explain it, but he just seems to have more life, more of an "affect," I think you psychiatrists call it. Jake sometimes seems like two different people—no, make that several different people: a playful, adventuring bear on summer camping vacations; a morose, sullen child on Monday mornings; a shy, self-conscious adolescent at formal gatherings where he doesn't know many people; a warm, sensitive adult when a poem or movie or experience happens to touch him deeply; a spoiled, narcissistic child when I have not had time to cook a dinner and dessert; an old miser anxious to avoid the ravages of another economic depression when he even thinks about spending more than a dollar; a beautiful soul, open and giving and laughing when he feels secure in a small group of friends or family or alone with me.

Do you know all these sides of him, doctor? Can you possibly, I wonder? At first, this Christmas, I thought it was the baby—that he is feeling so proud of being a father—and I guess that does have something to do with it. He is an adult, an authority of his own. But it's more than having his own child. He just seems more relaxed, more secure, more—I just don't know the right words. For me it is all summed up in watching Jake talk to my father, talking about Medicare, about society's problems or golf or the baby or comparative gas mileage—nothing earthshaking, but just finally talking like two adult human beings. How very much I'd like them to like each other.

So! As I said, today I am feeling benevolent toward you for whatever part you have played in this metamorphosis. I may yet have a leap of faith into Freudian techniques!

Sincerely,
JEANNE DANIELS

January 5

DEAR DR. FRICKMAN,

I'm writing this at 2:00 A.M. Consider this a retraction of any rash compliments I may have distributed earlier. I have one short question to insert into your busy schedule: How can such a miserly tightwad as my husband pay you so much money and not get better? Someone who worries about cash as much as he does should surely be trying to get his money's worth, right? Why is he perpetually on a diet and never losing weight? (The question is rhetorical, not physiological or even psychological. The answer: He eats constantly, diet or no diet. You should have seen him over Christmas vacation, especially at his mother's.) Why is he always saying we don't have enough of a social life, and then when we go out to one of my friends' houses, he acts like I'm dragging him to cruel and unusual punishment? Why does he enthusiastically endorse or initiate a plan to have friends to dinner and promise to help with preparations and then run out to play hours of tennis or handball while I run around madly cleaning house, taking care of the baby, and trying to cook the meal? Let's face it: His decision-making powers

leave something to be desired. I don't understand how he could be
paying you so much and getting so little. Jake is like a two-year-old
in a toy store—unable to decide on what he really wants or even
likes. I would have thought *this* problem would have some solution
after all this time. I'll admit there have been changes, but oh, what
a slow process is change!

Well, while we're on the topic of money, I might as well bring
up the phone bills. Does that sound trivial and banal to you, highly
paid professional that you are? Well, even to me, underpaid mother,
wife, maid, cook, laundress, nurse—and, alas, student and all-
around-servant—even to so lowly a one as me it sounds trivial and
banal. Ah! But not so to your word-constipated, penny-pinching
patient. Oh, no. To him the subject of phone bills calls forth loud
and resonant tones. He's highly critical of my calling my brother
in Boston or my old college friend in New York State. A postage
stamp is much cheaper, says he. With that I must agree. I only
wonder why he doesn't apply that rule to his analysis. Just think,
he could write you letters like I do for only fifteen cents a day
instead of thirty dollars a day. We could buy stock in the phone
company with the money we would save.

Listen: It's just not fair, and I wish you'd tell him so. After all,
if he's not going to be part of my life, I've got to have *someone* to talk
to. I need to talk to people, my friends, my family. I am becoming
entirely alienated from the group down here. So what if I make a
few calls to old friends, my mother and father, even Jake's sister? I
don't spend in a *whole month* of long-distance calls what he spends
in one day of analysis! There is no justice. It is not fair for him to
have someone to talk his problems over with five days a week, week
in and week out (month in and month out, year in and year out,
decade in and decade out) and me to have to feel guilty after I've
passed the first three minutes of a telephone call. *I'm telling you that
he rants and raves over the phone bill!* He wants *me* to economize—as
if I were living in a mansion with a closet full of clothes, with a
housekeeper, a baby-sitter, gourmet dinners, and fine furniture. *I
need to talk to friends*—even if he doesn't. (Don't take that personally.)
Please make him understand that. I need to be dependent sometimes
too, even if he refuses to believe that. I need empathy and warmth
and support like any normal human being. Can an analyst really do

that for anyone? Since Jake can only give me such gifts sometimes (and never can I actually count on him), I must depend on my close friends and family. And none of them sits there saying "Um-hmmmm" noncommittally, and none answers my questions with *more* questions. Your process of psychoanalysis is really so cold. If Jake only knew better how to give and receive empathy and warmth, he wouldn't be going to your isolation booth every day.

Emphatically,
JEANNE DANIELS

January 8

DEAR DR. FRICKMAN,

Call him off! Now we're back to too much sex again. Isn't there a happy medium? Why is Jake always, with everything, at one extreme or the other? I mean, he's either gorging himself on coffee cakes and licorice and spicy meatball submarine sandwiches, *or* he's eating only a two-inch cube of cheddar cheese with a glass of water as his day's food ration. He's either full of energy, playing three straight sets of tennis and eager to go out to one of those macho, action-packed movies afterwards, *or* he's grouchy and falls asleep in front of the TV after five minutes of "Kojak" or "Columbo." He's either kind and gentle, cajoling me to go out for a walk or a ride or to read to him, *or* he's withdrawn and silent and ready to bite me if I ask the wrong question. We've tried talking about these ex-tremes, and when he's in a communicative mood he tells me directly that it has nothing to do with me, that I'm not responsible for how he's feeling on any particular day, that I shouldn't let it bother me. Nothing to do with me, indeed! I *live* with him, and his mood affects me, affects *us*. Although, I must say that I do find life easier now knowing he can go work it out with you, that he may snap out of one of his downs, his depressions, by talking to you. I'm beginning to dread it when you take a day or a week off. I usually find out because he is behaving differently and I ask him if he's seen you. I've even learned to do this in a casual manner, the way some men ask if a woman is in a bitchy mood because of being on the rag or some such vulgarity—so he doesn't get angry. He *won't* bite me after all.

Bonnie has settled down to sleeping for longer periods at night and to taking almost predictable naps both morning and afternoon. So I've been able to work a bit on my dissertation.

But now I have a new crisis on my hands, and I think I even have to ask you for your help—quite seriously, humbly, without sarcasm. The English department has offered me a full-time instructorship beginning next week. Someone fell ill and has taken a leave of absence. I am frantic over making this decision, and Jake is not helping a bit. He doesn't even understand why I'm agonizing over it. Taking the job has several advantages: money (much better than part-time pay); experience, which is good just for the experience and also for obtaining a job in the future; an outlet for me, a chance to get out of the house and share with friends once again. But there are disadvantages too: I'm still nursing Bonnie, she doesn't take a bottle, I don't think I can give her up to a sitter several days a week —besides *who* would be good enough, etc.; I still haven't finished my dissertation; and Jake doesn't want me to, for a whole list of his own reasons, I suppose—mostly, he doesn't want me to leave the baby at all. I feel like I've stumbled—or have been pushed—onto the crossroads between my two worlds, and I'm being pulled with equal force in two opposite directions. I can't believe how utterly incapable of making this decision I seem to be, and I have to let the secretary know by tomorrow.

Help! What really upsets me is that Jake hardly sees this as worth talking about; he thinks I should stay home with Bonnie and that's that. I do too, in a way. But he makes me feel that I am trapped, that I have no other choice, that I'll be a failure of a mother if I don't stay here twenty-four hours a day. Wait, let me guess what you're thinking—that this is all projection, that no one can make me feel such and such (Jake reiterates this point often, presumably direct from the horse's mouth—you, that is), that one must be responsible for one's own decisions. . . . OK, OK. But I'm stuck; I can't make a decision right now. And Jake's not helping, and it's not fair. We both have a baby and only my time and schedule have to be juggled around. My whole entire life is different, night and day, while he goes on as before—to analytic hour, to the hospital, home to a prepared dinner, clean clothes, an occasional game of handball or even tennis if the temperature gets to forty-five degrees (can you imagine them playing out in the cold like that?), to study or read or watch TV, and then to bed for an uninterrupted full night's sleep (he doesn't even know that I may be up three times in the night, sometimes, for over an hour).

So what do I do? Stay home and hope for a job next time? What if I say no too often? What if no one takes me seriously as a scholar any more? What if I get labeled as a housewife who teaches an occasional course in English composition, the one who never quite finished her dissertation after a promising stint as a graduate student? *Or,* do I try to find a baby-sitter and plunge into this job? What if Bonnie won't take a bottle from anyone and only wants to nurse and I can't be there? What if I am regarded—by others and by myself—as a negligent mother? What if I start to feel that someone else has raised my child and I'll be sorry I missed out on being with her? Just thinking about her now makes my milk let down. I can't leave her, I know I just can't do it.

What do you think?
JEANNE

January 13

DEAR DR. FRICKMAN,

You've got to *do something* about this. Jake is trying to force me into being *his* mother again. And *I can't do it* anymore. He's regressing; please, dear God, not now! I have this baby now and I have not had more than four straight, uninterrupted hours of sleep in over three months. I worry about nursing and diaper rash and vomiting —sometimes I feel overwhelmed at the huge responsibility I have for this tiny person. Until just recently I was going up to check her breathing if she had slept more than three hours; I read the La Leche League books to be sure to do the best I can with nursing; I read Dr. Spock on cradle cap and on spoiling a baby; I read Brazelton's *Infants and Mothers* to anticipate what happens next in the precious life of my little Bonnie; I've painted bright shapes on her walls and ceiling and bought a colorful mobile for over her crib; I bought a baby-food grinder so that when she's ready for solids I will not have to give her store-bought baby food with all those sugar and salt additives. My days, my weeks, my life revolve around this baby. I've tried to include Jake, to get him to care about the rash on her face and to get him involved in feeding her a relief bottle and rocking her to sleep in his arms. He acts like he's afraid to touch her if she's crying, and he insists that I'm the one she *wants* when she fusses. Oh, he likes to coo over her when she's content, but he doesn't want anything to do with the actual, everyday care of her. Why? I don't understand. I don't understand. He *is* a tender person under all that virile, macho exterior, I *know* he is.

If you haven't already guessed, this is a complaint letter, doctor, a crotchety, cranky, complaint—from a tired, confused mother who, it seems, has two children instead of one. He absolutely expects me to carry on as I did before the baby, to make his desserts and type his letters and have his laundry clean and folded in his drawer when he needs it. My dissertation is not even considered by him; he does not seem to take my intellectual goals seriously—even though we've lived on my intelligence (in the form of fellowship and assistantship money) for these three years and more. I lead an unbelievably schizophrenic life writing a few pages of my dissertation at nap times and then cleaning shitty diapers or reading Dr. Spock or dressing up the baby for an outing during the rest of the day—not to mention housework and laundry and dinner and any extra chores Jake may think up for me. And then, I'm supposed to be *La Dolce Vita* in bed. And in two days I begin teaching a night course—my solution to the problem I wrote you about last time, by the way—one night a week.

I'm tired. I'm exhausted. There are too many demands being made on me. You MUST get Jake to understand that I cannot mother him any longer and that he has to become a more involved father. He wanted this baby as much as I did. *What is his problem?* I need real help for one evening a week and he is refusing. Help.

Sincerely,

J——

January 19

Dear Dr. Frickman,

Oh fine! Now he's become an amateur psychiatrist (as if he wasn't bad enough off already with all this constant introspection) after only three days on a psychiatry rotation; lectures or seminars and some clinical observation and experience are to be included. Already he's practicing on me. Yesterday I had a particularly difficult day with Bonnie, who seems to have had a slight reaction to an immunization shot. I'd been carrying her around almost all day, trying to keep the poor little thing comfortable, and by 6:30 when Jake came in we were both exhausted. Right off the bat he asks me, "What does 'A stitch in time saves nine' mean?" I looked at him blankly and sat down to try to quiet Bonnie by nursing her again. Nonplussed, he says, "Well, then, what does 'A rolling stone gathers no moss' mean?" I racked my tired brain to find a connection between these proverbs and my screaming child—I actually thought he was making some obscure criticism of my child-care ability. Or was he perhaps referring to a shirt I hadn't sewn a button on? Or was he announcing his intention to leave—to get rolling and gather no moss, so to speak? I felt like screaming and only thought better of it because Bonnie was finally relaxing in my arms and looking drowsy as she nursed. Jake pushed me for an answer, so as calmly as possible I said I didn't know. "Ah-humm," he said gently, with an intonation which I consider appropriate to (or peculiar to, anyway) a psychiatrist. And then he turned and went upstairs to change clothes. Much later, over our dinner of cheese omelets, he explained that he was testing me for schizophrenia by asking me the meaning of those proverbs, and again he pushed me for an answer! I flatly refused; I do believe he doesn't know what they mean himself and was hoping to catch me in the same way. I told him to shut up and enjoy his omelet because a bird in the hand is worth two in the bush and it's not a good idea to put all your eggs in one basket and anyway, people in glass houses shouldn't throw stones. He smiled; not a giggle or a laugh, but at least he smiled, so I did take hope.

Now! I've been really quite startled by a sudden realization that I must share with you. You must be reading these letters after all, or, even if you're not, I have to give you credit for being more perceptive than I had thought. I'm beginning to see that if I bitch loudly enough about some injustice or whatever, Jake is bound to bring it up in analysis and work out a solution, even do a complete turnabout on a given disagreement. For example: my taking on this night course. We spent *hours* arguing about whether or not I could or should or would do it and over whether he could, should, or would take care of Bonnie one evening a week. He was dead set against it, no matter what arguments, no matter what pleas I made, so I made arrangements for a baby-sitter. I was pretty convinced that it wasn't me he was worried about, or even Bonnie (which he pretended); I knew he didn't want the responsibility of taking Bonnie one night a week. I had bitched and explained how much I needed to be out a little on my own doing something with adults, and I pointed out that he could cut down on handball or tennis for a semester to become acquainted with his daughter. Nothing doing, *until* he saw you and apparently talked about it, and called me midmorning from the hospital to tell me to go ahead and teach if I really wanted to and that I could count on him to take care of Bonnie. I was so taken aback that at first I didn't believe him, so he went on to say, in a rarely communicative moment, that he wanted me to be happy and he thought it would be better for all of us if I could do what I wanted and not worry about Bonnie. I had such an impulse to call you when I hung up the phone after Jake's call. How do you accomplish these things? Phenomenal!

David came over to talk that same day, in the afternoon after clinic. He and Pamela live in their own apartment now (and two other dental students live with Timothy next door), so I don't get to see David too often unless the four of us get together for a movie or whatever. He doesn't talk directly about anything, so I have to do most of the talking and ask questions so that he can talk about what is bothering him. I tried telling him about my conflict between the wish to be a perfect mother and the wish to be a brilliant scholar. He was so bitingly cynical, and so coldly rejecting of the little girl I held closely in my arms, that he made me feel extremely depressed. Is this an unresolvable conflict, after all? My good friend David, why does he want to be so discouraging? He's so down on the whole idea of marriage and especially of children . . . and yet I wonder if he'll be happy in his career either? He sure is searching for something. Despite my conflict, I somehow feel that I'm several steps ahead in the search. And even Jake, Jake too can find more to be positive about than David. You may actually be helping that man grow up—but I doubt it. If he keeps up with his amateur psychiatrist act, you can just bet that I'll begin throwing a lot of stones through the delicate and fragile glass house he has built up with your help.

Very sincerely,

JEANNE DANIELS

January 30

DEAR DR. FRICKMAN,

Bonnie and I, my dracaena, four philodendrons, three wandering Jews, two spider plants, one pepperomia—altogether, seventeen assorted green plants from my home—are resting peacefully here in Pamela and David's apartment. Ours is being debugged, you know, fogged out with some noxious substance, so we have to stay out of it for five hours. The man with the mask said my plants would be OK, but I hated to leave them. Can you believe it, that after all this time I am going to be able to open a cabinet or to turn on a light at night without seeing these atrocious bugs scurry to escape? I want you to know that I boldly wrote out a check for twenty-five dollars for this service, and I do not feel one bit, not one iota, guilty. Now how did I come to this wonderful decision? Do you think Jake finally relented—got sick and tired of bugs and decided it could be worth twenty-five dollars to be rid of them? No, no, nothing as drastic as that.

Well, let me free associate here a bit and explain to you how it is that I come to be sitting here grinning and thinking about all those little roaches dropping dead at this very moment in their hiding places behind the woodwork.

It all started with a book we read for my women's book group last week, Margaret Atwood's *Surfacing.* It's about a young woman who returns to a childhood home in the Canadian woods; she relives some scenes of her childhood (in such ways as looking through old scrapbooks and working in the old garden), searches for her missing father and, finally, discovers him dead, drowned in the lake. Now what, you might ask, could that have to do with me and our roaches? A major theme of the book, put into words by the protagonist near the end, is: "This above all, to refuse to be a victim. Unless I can do that I can do nothing." It doesn't seem like much of a resolution at first glance, and some members of the book group thought it hardly worth writing such a book about. But I found it provocative, positively freeing, enlightening. *That's* what it's all about. To take charge of your own life—to refuse to be a victim. When the woman protagonist was a child she drew pictures of Easter eggs with fantasy scenes in them while her brother drew war planes with swastikas. She was, even then, choosing victim imagery (Easter, death of an innocent Jew) while her brother was choosing quite the opposite, the imagery of victimizers, of murderers who rationalized the death of innocent millions.

Women are too often brought up with the idea that they cannot take control of their own lives. Perhaps it is true for many men as well, but the point is that it need not be like that. Well, to make a long story short, I was awestruck by the theme in the book, and I thought, here I am getting my Ph.D., raising a child, caring for a home, thinking I have such control over my life. Then why am I doing something so dumb as living with roaches when I could easily be rid of them (well, not easily, perhaps, but it's certainly possible anyway)? I mean, I've sprayed, bitched, screamed, complained, sprayed again—all to no avail. So—why not take real control of the situation? I mean, what's the worst that could happen? Jake may yell; he certainly won't hit me; he can't take away my allowance ($0.00)—and the bugs will be gone! I've got nothing to lose but a houseful of bugs.

Another association on this same subject: Genny, my old college friend, sent me a beautifully illustrated book of fairy tales and rhymes that I haven't thought about in years. Did you ever realize how many *victims* there are in fairy tales? Snow White, who bites that apple without thinking out the ramifications of the situation; Hansel and Gretel, who do their best not to be victims first of their stepmother and then of the wicked witch in the candy house; Cinderella, who lets herself be mistreated by her stepmother and stepsisters and then passively allows herself to be pushed into marriage just because a shoe happens to fit her foot (it's OK if you believe in happily-ever-after of course, but what if the prince decides he needs analysis?); and in Rumpelstiltskin that poor girl is a victim of her father, who uses her for his own means. Fairy-tale land is full of such stories, absolutely full of people allowing themselves to become victims instead of taking control over their lives.

Oh—and one further association, since I've already rambled on this far. Actually, this is a bit of wonderful news for me; my paper on literary suicides has been accepted for publication in a literary journal! I'm ecstatic, and yet my reaction is a mixed one because this acceptance comes at a time when I'm sick of this whole suicide study —more *victims* who have gone so far that they are unable to turn themselves around and take control. I sympathize, but I grow impatient. I want to know more about women who didn't let themselves become victims, who didn't just sink into complaining and bitching and then passive acceptance of circumstances. What about the women who had children *and* were or are active in lives of their own—George Sand, Charlotte Perkins Gilman, Tillie Olsen, Margaret Drabble? There must be many more I know nothing about. That will be my next project—maybe I'll write up an outline and apply for a grant.

Jake is into his own research these days. I am amazed at the report he has prepared for a psychiatry seminar—about Dr. Thomas Szasz who, it seems to me, practically denies the very existence of psychiatric illness. Is this a good thing for Jake to be doing—straying outside the boundaries of the Freudian system, questioning its basic assumptions? Well, it sounds healthy to me, but I assume you may see it in terms of "acting out," perhaps repeating a pattern of rebellion against authority, something like that. The Freudian system is, as far as I'm concerned, a circle; it's got you coming and going, no matter what you do or don't do, even though, as I've just read, Freud himself said that sometimes a cigar is only a cigar. That's just because he smoked them. Ironic that the cigar was instrumental in his death, isn't it? Kind of like the snake devouring its own tail, one endless circle.

Best,
JEANNE DANIELS

February 4

DEAR DR. FRICKMAN,

So . . . I knew this was coming, knew as certainly as I knew I
was going to catch the chicken pox because I had spent every afternoon for two weeks playing in the sandbox or riding tricycles with
my friend Mickey, who one day appeared at his window with funny
red spots all over his tearful face. I *knew* Jake was going to start
suggesting analysis for me. I saw this coming for a long time, but
I'm still wondering about the specific dynamics of it. I can't get a
straight answer out of Jake, but there can only be a limited number
of reasons why he would recommend or suggest such folly to me:
most obvious, misery loves company; he's convinced I'm schizoid if
not actually schizophrenic; he wants to keep you psychiatrists living
high (and us low); all of the above. Have I missed something? Or am
I simply avoiding something?

Anyway, he's now become a real born-again Freudian (has a
nice ring to it, doesn't it). Alleluia! Alleluia! The gospel according
to Freud: In the beginning was sex and aggression (and maybe the
search for pleasure and the seeking of one's own death). And lo, a
new prophet came out of the tribes of Israel to speak of the conflicts
represented by id, ego, superego. He spoke and wrote many words.
And the words became flesh and grew beards and went out to all
people (who had enough money to spend a fortune being introspective and childish).

Thank you, but I have neither the time, the money, nor even
the inclination to become so self-absorbed, so self-indulgent. Not
that it hasn't done worlds of good for Jake. Don't think I'm putting
you down for a moment. But it's not for me, no way. Jake assures
me that if I only truly understood the process, I would welcome the
opportunity (welcome the opportunity to suffer? to sacrifice?—
sounds familiar somehow). Well that's just the same old thing. One
has to be "motivated" to do well in analysis, right? Yep—just like
that old line to the sinners, the real down-and-outers who are led
to feel the *need* for salvation. One big switch on the psychoanalytic
path to grace, however. The poor man may as well try to ride a '57
Chevy pickup truck through the eye of a needle, for it is the man

in the new Mercedes who is accepted for the grace of the healing powers.

Now I don't want you to think that I think I'm perfect. By no means. I have problems—"pathology," to use your terminology— like everyone else. I mean, for example, sometimes I really do feel like I may have a tendency to being schizoid. For instance, the other night we were invited to Evelyn and Michael's apartment for din- ner. David and Pamela were there, and Timothy and Holly (his newest girl friend.) As we sat around, getting high, gorging our- selves on Evelyn's carefully prepared food, I had this sense, this kind of double feeling, of being there both as a full participant, talking, laughing, eating, listening to and making inane observa- tions and meaningless comments about the state of the world or a book or the politics of the university . . . *and* as a nonparticipant, a silent self standing apart trying to figure out why each person (including my other self) said this or that, and to whom and what it might all mean, not judging or pitying or ridiculing or praising, but merely observing, wondering. How much there is to under- stand; how little of the iceberg of self does anyone allow to show above the surface. And in a group, all these individuals behave so unlike how they do when I see them individually and we talk about far less important issues—less important in the greater world, that is; far more important to those individuals, of course. So maybe that is my pathology, this sense of doubleness. But I think I can live with it.

Sincerely,
JEANNE

February 15

DEAR DR. FRICKMAN,

"Daffodils—that come before the swallows dare, / And take the winds of March with beauty."

It's Shakespeare, from a play that Jake and I read together ages ago, the summer we met, in fact. Do you believe that yesterday he brought home a beautiful bunch of daffodils and a valentine card in which he had written Shakespeare's lines! I cried, I just cried. You see what a caring, beautiful man is there inside, a man imprisoned by the traditions and conventions of our society, trapped into feeling that he must always appear a cool, macho, almost unemotional character? He's wonderful, you're wonderful, life is wonderful! Wait, wait, let us not become hysterical. . . . But I am truly pleased. You know, this all makes me wonder about why I have such a wish for this romantic kind of behavior. What is it in me that needs such demonstrations of affection? Does it mean I'm insecure? Unfulfilled? Adolescent? Unrealistic? Superficial? Melancholic? Why do I find a sense of almost painful joy looking at this splash of yellow flowers on this dreary, gray February day, wishing myself into Shakespeare's lines, into being, myself, one of the daffodils "that come before the swallows dare, / And take the winds of March with beauty"? I have a feeling that this would be looked upon as a character defect of some sort by you and your comrades. I mean, to be overtly emotional, to show one's deep feelings is dangerous, hysterical, or some such term. And to defend one's right to both the feelings and the display of them is also dangerous, indicative of deep depression, perhaps. Well, maybe so—maybe I should fit your labels, for whatever they're worth, but somehow I feel that my life is just as worth living as the lives of you bearded puppets and your disciples. (Tsk! Hostile too!)

Indeed, the world is full of fine, exciting, *un*analyzed people, good old neurotics who make life interesting, who add their energies to social, cultural, intellectual, technological activities, and any other area you can think of. The composition class I'm teaching evenings is made up, mostly, of older students, men and women who are coming back to school for a variety of reasons and from a variety of backgrounds; there are several housewives (who view the newer term "homemaker" with disdain), a salesman, a telephone lineman, a lab technician, two secretaries, several other businessmen, a physician, and a few "regular" college students, two of whom are working in the daytime to pay for their educations. This class is so different from other composition courses I've taught, not only because it's at night and we meet only once a week and for a longer period of time (three hours), but because these people seem so much more interested in getting in touch with the rest of the class, in learning about and learning from each other. One big problem in teaching freshman composition is finding ways to motivate students to write, to interest them in writing about something, anything. They so often seem to think that writing a composition means turning out a little ego piece on "What I did over summer vacation" or "What I want to be when I grow up." I am often amazed at their lack of interest in even the most commonly discussed issues, such as abortion, human rights, the ERA, or environmental protection. But these older students have little problem finding a topic to write about; what's most exciting to me is that they spur each other on to agree or disagree with one another. I've become more of a mediator than a teacher. After my short lecture on grammar or construction (and even there, they are motivated to learn on their own), I throw the evening open to class readings or discussion and criticism. They point out to each other where the logic of a certain paper fails, and are even able to suggest, at times, what would improve the opening or the closing of a given composition. At the risk of sounding hysterical again—I love them. I have learned so much from this small group of people and have learned so much about them from what each has said or written. And yet so many of them have, it seems, put me on some kind of pedestal simply because I'm The Instructor, as if I have some magical knowledge that they lack.

Freud knows I certainly don't feel magical these days. Between caring for Bonnie (and Jake), housekeeping, teaching, and writing, I have little time for painted wings and dragon wings. Alas, I've become a real grown-up, I guess. Pamela came over this morning, her day off, to ask me about David, about whether I could help her understand his behavior. The only magic I had, woefully inadequate, was listening; fortunately that's all she really wanted from me. So Bonnie and I listened, and I truly did feel old, not old enough to have gained wisdom about these things, but old enough to know that we all have our little patterns to exist within, patterns that imprison us and make us repeat past feelings and thoughts and actions. I see, pretty clearly I think, Pamela's patterns, and David's patterns. I can even see how they intersect, mesh together here at this edge or there at the core. But I have no crystal ball. Do *you*, Dr.

Frickman? Do you sit there in your office diagramming the patterns of your patients, perhaps trying to break the patterns? Once again, I cannot resist asking, what about the other patterns—the ones that your patients have matched up with their own? What about my patterns—and Bonnie's patterns, which are just now being formed? Don't you think that what you are doing may endanger those of us who do not particularly want our patterns tampered with?

Oh, I didn't mean to get into this attitude again. After all, I'm delighted at Jake's pattern break—at his wonderfully thoughtful and romantic gift of daffodils. I am hopeful; perhaps we shall have an early spring, a field of golden daffodils. . . .

Regards,
JEANNE

February 18

JOHN FRICKMAN

AM AT DEATH'S DOOR WITH FLU STOP BABY SICK TOO STOP JAKE DENYING AND PLAYING TENNIS ELKINS PARK COURTS STOP DO SOMETHING STOP OR ELSE STOP

JEANNE DANIELS

Part Four

February 23

DEAR DR. FRICKMAN,

FINISHED! I have finally written the last words of my dissertation, have dealt with the suicides of Virginia Woolf and Sylvia Plath and the tragic death of Zelda Fitzgerald, and laid them all to rest. I don't know when I've felt such relief—it's like finally pushing that baby's head through, though not exhilarating in quite the same way. And there is still plenty of work to do—revising, checking it all out with my dissertation committee, getting it typed, working out technical details of footnotes and quotations, but it *is* finished. Down at the library the other night, before class, I looked at several dissertations to see how people had handled acknowledgments, dedications, that sort of thing. Many male graduate students have hailed the unceasing patience or unfailing aid of their wives for either typing or merely being somehow supportive through their ordeal. And a few female graduate students have also dedicated their pedantic volumes to their husbands or to parents or even children. No way am I going to thank Jake for all his help and understanding.

What really gets me is that I'm supposed to carry on with everything no matter what he does or how he behaves and no matter what I may be feeling—even if I'm sick, like the other day. (Next time I'll send a singing telegram messenger so I can at least find out your response.) I mean, to Jake I am never sick. What if I get really sick? What if I need surgery—neurosurgery? If I had a brain tumor growing out through my scalp, he'd say it's nothing. Now take these terrible headaches I've been getting lately. He does pretend some clinical interest to show off his knowledge of neurology (what kind of pain, which side, follow my finger with your eyes), and then always puts me off with the two-aspirin routine. No help. No help at all.

Although today, Sunday, he did get up with Bonnie at 6:30 and took care of her all morning while I wrote the last few paragraphs of my dissertation. This came about as a result of last week's revolution—the day Bonnie and I were sick and the doctor went off to play tennis. I feel confident that you must have heard about the war we waged over that. It's probably just as well you didn't respond to my telegram directly; Jake seems to have worked out something since then because this morning's arrangement was entirely his idea. He only asked me where Bonnie's undershirts are and must he really feed her cereal and how do you make it, anyway? I think this kind of thing may be good for all of us—for me, for Jake, for Bonnie.

So now it's on to a new project. I have this wonderful idea for a book, a kind of scholarly-popular book maybe titled something like "Mothers as Artists"—no more of these pitiful, childless suicide reiterations. This book will be about people like George Sand (two children), Tillie Olsen (four children), Mrs. Gaskell (two or three or more, including a son who died in infancy), Margaret Drabble (three children), Harriet Beecher Stowe (seven children). We women need to know more about possible role models; enough of these morbid genius types. They have their place as much as the male genius types, but we need not dwell on them. We need to know more about all the possibilities open to us, to make our own definitions of successful and fulfilled lives as mothers and/or artists and/or anything we may choose. I'm going to make up an outline and apply for a grant to write this book. With my published paper and now my completed dissertation, *someone* might be interested. I plan to research out not only the great mother-artists of the past, but contemporary writers and maybe mothers in other fields too, like Margaret Mead or Karen Horney. Think of the possibilities!

But alas! Right now Bonnie needs me. She is growing more beautiful everyday (a line right out of those fairy-tale stories about princesses, but she truly *is*), and I find I am thrilled to have finished the dissertation so I can focus most of my energy on her. She's my little pal now, really starting to reach out into the world around her. I wish you could see her——

Sincerely,
JEANNE

February 27

DEAR DR. FRICKMAN,

As usual, I am one day late with news that Jake must have already told you, but by now you must know that we often have very different thoughts and feelings about anything that comes up, and I figure you may as well hear both sides. And this, *can* you wonder how I feel about this?

HOORAY! HIP, HIP, HOORAY! California here we come. My heart is already in San Francisco. So this is really it, Dr. Frickman; we'll really be leaving you. And I want you to know that Jake has made this decision quite without pressure from me. When the acceptance came he asked me what I thought. We had a long discussion about professional opportunities for both of us. I hated to bring it up, but I *had* to ask about whether he could really leave you and Analysis. He just smiled and said that there are analysts in San Francisco. (Now how does *that* make *you* feel? I refuse to even think about that; I'm too happy!) And then he said that he had been thinking a great deal about it, and that if I agreed, we would go to San Francisco! I feel so deliciously wicked, the wicked fairy who banished the analyst from the kingdom—hmmm, might have possibilities for a new fairy tale. I wish I had been there to hear him tell you about it. Or did you expect this? Right now I'm going to go and put the triumphant march from *Aida* on the stereo and turn it up all the way and listen to it six times through!

Sincerely,
JEANNE

March 3

DEAR DR. FRICKMAN,

I could spit. I could just spit. Like a cat, or a snake, or any angry, cornered animal. How in the world did I allow myself to get into this corner? And *you*, I can't believe *you* are going to allow this. Of all things—a trip to Florida for a crash course in scuba diving. I have to pinch myself to be convinced that this is really happening. And it's not just that Bonnie and I are being left behind. He's always yelling so much about money, and I've economized to the point of absurdity (to pay *your* bill I might add) and now he's going to take a spring vacation, by himself no less, as if he's the only one who's been working hard, poor dear, and deserves a break. Mandy is angry with Sydney over this bright idea too (as you must know, Sydney's going too) but at least she hasn't been skimping to pay for analysis.

Where were you last week, by the way? You go away for one week and Jake falls apart. Oh, wonderful! This is definite regression, back to the selfish, narcissistic, macho character, back to square one, Dr. Frickman. Over two years of analysis adding up to only a lot of wasted money. Good God, what is life going to be like when Jake doesn't have you to talk to anymore?

I could spit. I feel almost speechless.

I could just spit!

Well, fortunately I'm off that merry-go-round of illusion; I was really beginning to think that Jake had changed, that there was hope for him yet, but that was idiotic. I was fooled; I was a fool. No way could I ever now endorse this expensive nonsense. Am I supposed to be happy that he is forming friendships, that he is expanding his world, that he is becoming independent, that he is going back to the womb (ocean)? Oh sure, that's probably one way to look at it. Well, let me not interfere in this glorious process, the growth of the self, but be sure that I'm not sticking around to be pushed into the corner by it. Trapped.

Yesterday afternoon I had a bit of regression myself—not that I'm apologizing for it. Timothy, dear sexy Timothy, came over while Bonnie was napping to borrow a clove of garlic and, as we got talking, he invited me to go for a "spin" in his new TR-7. I was able to get Eleanor, a widow who lives in our apartment building and who baby-sits for us occasionally, to come up to stay with Bonnie, and I went out for a ride in Timothy's yellow sports car. Instant fantasy. All the sexual fantasies that have hardly entered my head in months and months came flooding back during that hour's ride around town. For one isolated hour I thought nothing about taking care of anyone or anything but myself, of caring only about how *I* feel. It was fun and free and without responsibility, exhilarating, exciting, pleasurable and . . . unrealistic. I'm not part of that world anymore; I've grown up. I can enjoy it still for what it's worth, but I can no longer convince myself that it is reality, "where it's at," as its proponents might say. I *want* my responsibilities now, my child, my home, my teaching; those are all choices I've consciously made. But my husband, your patient—what kind of commitment can I maintain if he is to remain in that adolescent world? It's not fair— oh, how that echoes my own small self as a child when my older brother got to do something I couldn't. Maybe that's how you'll interpret all of this—back to penis envy?

Scuba diving. I could spit.

I could just spit.

I can't even go on with this letter!

JEANNE DANIELS

March 10

DEAR DR. FRICKMAN,

OK. So I'm not so angry anymore. Actually, this might be a good experience for Jake after all. I mean, I really *should* see a lot of positive potential in this bit of behavior; he's doing something with a friend, something that may be an adventure, something that is entirely different from medical school, tennis, or "Kojak," and he may find this a good opportunity for thinking about his own life away from both of us—you and me, I mean. And maybe he'll come back with a better attitude, in a better mood, after satisfying that search for excitement (or is it the wish to get back to the womb— and what better womb than the warm waters of the Florida Keys?).

I *still* think it's not fair to spend the money to go, and I'm still jealous at being left behind here to teach and take care of Bonnie, but I'm able to see the other side now. At least I'm not spitting anymore.

Actually, my whole mood is lifting because spring is finally coming to the dreary grayness of the city. The sycamores out front once again are alight with the soft greenness of spring buds, and the crocuses in our front patch of garden are poking up through the winter accumulation of leaves and rubbish. One day soon, when the sun halts the showers, Bonnie and I will go out and clean up the whole garden, rake and weed and let the new bright flowers breathe freely in the spring air. Bonnie's just about big enough for the back-pack now; I have to pack her in with a pillow and blankets so she is able to see the world in an upright position. She loves it! And with spring coming we are no longer so trapped in this damnable apartment. The other afternoon Bonnie and I took the bus and subway downtown to the art museum, and we had a wonderful time. I fed her a jar of sweet potatoes and some applesauce in the museum cafeteria and then nursed her to sleep in the women's lounge. By then we had already seen a great deal, so I just sat with her in my arms in front of a beautiful, very old Oriental tapestry, and I felt more contented than I have for a long time. I imagined myself, sitting there in my jeans and navy blue turtleneck, as some- how a cross between the smiling Buddha and the blessed Madonna, whose pictures I had been looking at all morning, sitting in an Oriental garden of paradise. Ah! Delusions of grandeur!

One other aspect of my life has opened up with some promise of sweetness and light. I almost hate to mention this after a long history of progressions and regressions, but I do believe that Jake's decision to move to San Francisco, and therefore terminate this analysis in June, has done more for him than all that has gone on in these two years and more. It's as if he finally decided to get serious, to quit fooling around, quit fooling himself. Take losing weight for example: He's been claiming to be trying to do it for as long as I can remember. He's always pretended that starving him- self most of the day is the answer—that anything stolen from the refrigerator after nine o'clock won't be considered in that big calo- rie counter in the sky. My Lord! In the past month he's been practically living on cheese with mustard, and coffee and water, with a hard-boiled egg (also with mustard) thrown in now and then. And he looks great. I've never seen such discipline in him. And you know, I realized with a real shock the other day that he no longer calls me Bitch when I bring up some point on which we disagree; I can't even remember the last time he spoke to me like that. So you see, all he really needed was to decide to break away from you, to make decisions on his own, to "get better" already. (How do you feel about that?) Now, if I ever went into analysis (purely a hypothetical supposition), you know what I'd do? For one thing, I'd welcome, invite, encourage Jake to come in to talk to my analyst if he felt he needed to; I wouldn't leave him out in the cold. And I'd make some kind of contract with my analyst—with planned mutual evaluation dates and a planned termination date. I mean, *why*, when what one is doing is trying to gain control of one's own life, *why* should one so completely give one's self up into the control of someone else? Oh, pooh, I'm not getting into psychoanalytic theory again.

Some interesting news: Evelyn thinks she is pregnant. Guess that's a good indication of how Michael did with his therapist and how Evelyn did with the burden of virginity. Of course this presents a new problem, although I think both will welcome it. Their apartment is filled with plants and cats, all *very* well cared for, as if they were children. You know the type, the nurturant intellectuals who expend their tenderness on flora and fauna. So spring has come to Evelyn and Michael too.

And my dear friend Randy in London—he too is feeling the excitement of spring. He visited Bloomsbury and sent me a gorgeous, short biography of Virginia Woolf filled with photographs and pictures of Virginia and many of the Bloomsbury Group. And his letter, a long, rambling one, had a kind of mystical tone to it, almost musical in the descriptions of the places he has been, the people he has met, his feelings about his own work, his own existence. Writing letters to him sometimes becomes strange—such intimacy, of a sort, with someone I hardly know. He has become, through the embroideries of my own lively fantasy, a symbol of all that is lacking in my relationship with Jake, and I find thinking about him almost painful.

But then, what shall I think of these letters I've been writing to you for almost a year and a half now, never hearing a word from you in response? Strange, isn't it, how you can be so much a part of my life—through Jake, I mean—and yet I know nothing about you. Sometimes I ask myself why I write these letters at all; it is certainly not an exaggeration to say that it is like talking to a blank wall. If I had been *saying* all I've written to someone—anyone— would my world now be different? But spring is here, and summer must then follow, and all this shall be ended, so why think about it?

Sincerely,
JEANNE

March 18

DEAR DR. FRICKMAN,

Two hours ago as I was happily bathing Bonnie, I had a call from a doctor in Florida, a doctor on board the *Valerie*, a navy ship which has a recompression chamber. "I'm calling for Jacob, your husband," he says as casually as possible. "He's had a diving accident." Like in the movies—and I felt like I was watching a movie, watching and listening to my calm self so slowly asking the right questions so neither the doctor nor my self would be put on the spot. Where is he now? What kind of accident? How serious? Could I talk with him? How is he now? Is his buddy Sydney there? What is your number there? Are you sure . . . ? All the answers calm and slow, professionally calm with no hint of panic. "He's in a recompression chamber here on board the *Valerie*. He seems to have let his air run too low and ascended holding his breath. No, not the bends, exactly. You can't talk to him, not because he can't talk but because there is no phone in there. He's looking pretty good now, but we can't tell yet how long we'll have to keep him in the chamber. Yes, his buddy is here; he said he'd call you in a half hour or so. Yes, I can give you the number here, Mrs. Daniels. There really seems to be no reason for alarm at this point; in fact, Jacob asked me to call you. . . ."

And three-quarters of an hour later, a sheepish call from Sydney. "Don't worry, Jeanne. We were scared at first, but the doc is doing fine now, don't worry." Obviously scared, voice shaking still. Like me. "He's doing good, Jeanne. I can see him in the chamber; the doctor went down with him to check him over; he looks like his usual cool self and the doctor says he is talking fine now. Well, he couldn't at first, when it first happened. No, not unconscious. . . . You know I'm not a doctor, Jeanne, I can't answer these kinds of questions. Yes, the doctor is still here. OK, let me see if he can come to the phone."

Official diagnosis: An air embolism paralyzed the right half of his body and made him unable to speak for a short time, like a stroke, but he seems fully recovered from those symptoms. Caused by holding breath when ascending. Air expands, enters pulmonary artery, travels to brain. Recompression to shrink air bubble, a precaution. A lucky man. An extremely lucky man.

Dr. Frickman! *Do you see what you let him get himself into?* Isn't this some terrible self-destructive tendency that you have chosen to ignore, to let him "act out," with your perfect nonintervention policy. Hell! I knew it! I knew this was a bad idea. They tell me that the *first* rule you learn in diving is never to hold your breath on ascending. Sydney even told me that that point had been stressed in their crash scuba course (which they finished just yesterday). So how can this "accident" be explained?

Oh my God, *is it me?* Is it my fault for pushing this idea of moving to San Francisco? For dragging him away from you? He doesn't want to leave you, does he? He's angry that you're not fighting to keep him here? He's angry with me because I want to move? He's trying to tell one of us something, right? He's not ready to cut the umbilical cord? As a result of analysis he doesn't need me anymore to mother him, but he has obviously transferred all that need to you? I feel so guilty.

I'm sitting here just waiting to hear from Sydney again. Bonnie is playing—sitting up on her own with pillows all around in case she should fall—and I'm just writing to you to take up time. I really feel like calling you, screaming at you. In fact, as soon as I hear from Sydney or the doctor *or* Jake, I *will* call you. I feel an explosion coming on.

JEANNE

March 22

DEAR DR. FRICKMAN,

Having Jake home again, after just five days away, is a curious mixture of pleasure and pain, like an intense physical relief. Do you know what I mean? Once I had a poison ivy rash all over me, and of course I wasn't supposed to scratch it. I tried not to, but when it just got too much to bear I would just scratch an arm or a leg as hard as I wanted to, rubbing away the itch from everywhere by concentrating on that one spot. The pleasure in that scratching was so intense that even knowing that pain would follow could not ruin it. Or it's like waiting a long time for a drink when you're extremely thirsty, when your body is practically crying out for water. Even as you finally drink, you have the feeling that by assuaging the intense thirst, by gaining this intense pleasure, you are taking away the possibility for a continuation of pleasure. I mean, it will be a long time before you're that thirsty again. And yet one's mouth and throat gulp down swallow after swallow to satisfy that thirst.

Once, Jake and I had the motorcycle up at Jake's mother's home, and although rain threatened we tried to ride back to the city. We spent an hour in a crummy garage somewhere about a half hour along the route, soaked and chilled, waiting for the rain to let up. It obviously wasn't going to let up for long. We decided to head back to his mother's rather than brave another hour and a half or more to the city. Well, a half hour in the rain on a motorcycle is like hell. The rain whips against your face, and your whole body tightens against the cold. I just hung on to Jake, hugging him as tightly as I could until we got back to his mother's house. And then there was only one bathtub in his mother's small home, and Jake decided over my halfhearted embarrassment (we hadn't been married more than a month or so), that we would get into a hot bath together. What an unbelievable pleasure to feel that hot water all over our goose-bumpy flesh, to let the water creep up and totally cover us, warming us in a pleasure that couldn't be spoiled even by knowing that it could only last for a few minutes. I mean, after five minutes, or perhaps less, a bath is a bath, pleasurable maybe, but not like when you first get in.

I guess that same mixture of intense physical pleasure and the pain of knowing that it must soon end is like an orgasm, that driving anticipation that cries out for a need to be satisfied; similar yet different from a poison ivy rash or a great thirst or a thoroughly chilled body. But again, that intense pleasure brings with it the pain of knowing that it can't last. All of this to explain how I feel about Jake's return—a return from death is not stretching words too far. He seems perfectly OK to me now, but oh, how much more precious, cherished. And you know, I think he feels the same way—not only about himself but about me and Bonnie as well. We just want to hug each other, not to think about how close he came to being lost, lost forever. O lost. *How would I live?*

While Jake was away for these few days, I got a lot done here. (Why is it so much easier to accomplish anything when he's not around?) My dissertation has been approved by the dissertation committee and I have only to go to an oral examination, which is more a formality than anything else, and then I shall have letters to put after my name as well. Big deal. Ah, but truly I feel this as a satisfying accomplishment. While Jake was gone I also managed to get my grant application completed, typed, and sent in just before the deadline.

So Jake is home, and Bonnie is the happiest, best baby in the world, and spring is here, and my life is easier than it has been for a long time, and we have the move to California to look forward to in June. So why am I feeling suddenly so . . . so scared? Maybe it's just the dream I had last night, a dream that was vaguely familiar and yet terrifying: I was hiking up a long green trail with Jake, a soft pine-needle trail lined by ferns and tall pine trees, and we were holding hands, listening for the sounds of the stream somewhere below the trail. And then the sound of water grew louder as we walked, and the trail was more open, less shaded by tall trees. We rounded a corner and were awestruck by a huge waterfall that sparkled with color and glowed with sunlight. And there were two men sitting on boulders beneath the falls; I couldn't get a good look at them, but I had the feeling that somehow you were there, and maybe my father, too. Both were dressed strangely in sort of flowing costumes, and they reminded me of the angels in Christ's tomb when the disciples looked in on Easter morning. But then the two figures faded, so after a while we decided to swim in the pond beneath the falls. We stripped down and entered the water together, happy at first, but then I grew terrified—not for any apparent reason, just trembling all over. Then . . . then I saw two bodies float out into the pond from under the falls, and I thought I saw blood seeping through the backs of their garments. I held on to Jake and began screaming, wildly, hysterically. That's how I woke up. . . .

And so today I'm afraid. Afraid that we shouldn't be moving, afraid—and I hate to write this—afraid that we shouldn't be leaving you. Not yet, anyway. Jake seems to feel fine about leaving; in fact he seems to feel better than ever about life, about himself. Then why do *I* feel like this? Oh, it must be that damned dream. Why must you haunt me even in dreams? I shall dress Bonnie up and take her to a concert in the park this afternoon and forget all this nonsense.

Meanwhile, don't go swimming in any mountain pools. . . .

JEANNE

April 2

DEAR DR. FRICKMAN,

Three in the morning and I can't sleep. No more nightmares, just wide awake. So I'm hoping that writing to you may help. I have a confession. Oh, I know you're not a priest or even my analyst, which would make it OK, I suppose. But you know, Dr. Frickman, over this long time I have sometimes felt that you were kind of my analyst too (I met someone at a party recently who is in training to become an analyst who *laughs* at that fantasy—but I am trusting you to understand) and sometimes I have felt that you were kind of like my father, and sometimes an imaginary, stern, nasty stepfather, and sometimes—like when Jake seems to have completely reversed himself on some issue—then I have even felt you to be some kind of god or at least a close, invisible ally. What lack is it in me that my fantasy of you fulfills—or partially fulfills? What is this emptiness I'm feeling? Don't you think it strange, absurd even, that we have never in all this time even been introduced to each other? I once saw the back of your head twenty rows in front of us at some psychoanalytic lecture at the medical school (Jake pointed you out but quickly and firmly ushered me out when the lecture was over!), and I've run into a couple of people who actually know you; one who was in the service with you for a couple years. To be frank, it is difficult for me to imagine you with a regular life of your own outside of analysis—as difficult as it was to believe that my parents engaged in sexual intercourse when I was first figuring out that kind of thing as a preadolescent! I know for a fact (a reliable source, as they say in the news business) that you have avoided attending several parties because we were going to be there. How realistic is that? How adult is that? I've never really understood the reason for this mystery, this intrigue almost! Oh, I have some vague idea about your theories of transference and all that. The longer I'm around in this psychiatric atmosphere (I mean getting to know other psychiatrists and talking to people in analysis), the more convinced I become that psychoanalysis is its own religion with its own god, its own saints —the Freudian apostles of the first generation—its own holy writ, canon law, and even a sort of clerical costume—the beard (I know you have one, I got that much out of Jake).

Ah! the confession. I'd almost forgotten. Since we will be moving in just two months now, I have had this determined desire to meet you or to at least *see* you face to face. Hmmm, interesting how words do come out of one's head: "Now we see as through a glass darkly, but then face to face"—as if you were indeed some god. I must really be in a twilight haze between waking and sleeping. Anyway, I have tried to catch sight of you at both your office locations, but have been, thus far, unsuccessful. Perhaps that is not to be. I certainly felt silly looking for you, and I doubt if I will try again. Even though I've never met you, Dr. Frickman, I shall miss you.

I think I'm tired enough now to go back to sleep.

Sincerely,
JEANNE

April 10

DEAR DR. FRICKMAN,

"April is the cruellest month, breeding / Lilacs out of the dead land, mixing / Memory and desire, stirring / Dull roots with spring rain." This April I think I finally understand what T. S. Eliot was writing about. My spirit, my soul, if you will allow the term, is stirring within me, vaguely aware of the winter's debris as well as the promises of spring. I have such mixed feelings about everything. But in the final analysis (no pun intended) I think things are finally looking up—for Jake, for me, for the two of us together. On Sunday we played tennis together in the afternoon after he had played for a couple hours in the morning with his tennis cronies. We haven't played together for such a long time, and the difference was startling. Jake's game, his strokes, his serve, have improved tremendously while I have fallen way behind and out of practice during the last year or so, because of, well, let's just say domestic and academic activities. So I expected that we would do worse than ever trying to play together (and it used to be just terrible, constant criticism from Jake). But quite the contrary, it was lovely—kind of low key, noncompetitive—and because of Jake's patient attitude I think I even did much better than when I played more often. We had Bonnie in a new jumper-walker that my folks bought for us. She sat in it on the sidelines eating Cheerios and making funny little sounds of happiness. A real family scene!

Later that evening, we joined Sydney and Mandy at their home for a takeout Chinese dinner. Sydney happened to mention the Florida trip and Jake's accident, and that led Jake into talking about it a little, certainly much more than I've heard him say about it since it happened. Did he tell you all about it in detail? I guess it quite frightened him; he remembers lying in a boat not being able to speak to tell anyone what was wrong, and not being able to move one side of his body. How absolutely terrifying—it reminds me of my childhood fears of being buried alive because no one would know I was merely in a coma. I do think that Jake views life differently now, not in any way I can explain clearly, but somehow quite differently. Do you feel it too?

Next weekend we're going for a bike ride down along the river.

Bonnie is quite comfortable in the backpack now and she'll ride in it on Jake's back. I'm holding my breath. Can this last? So much is happening so fast after all these slow, slow years.

JEANNE

April 23

DEAR DR. FRICKMAN,

Did you miss getting a letter from me last week? (I hope so, I do truly hope so.) I've been busy with teaching, which finishes up in a couple more weeks and with Bonnie, of course (surely six months is the most delightful age a child can be!), and with my friends and with some reading that I promised myself during all the time I worked on my dissertation—Proust, I've been immersed in Proust. And you must have heard about our day in New York City while my parents took care of Bonnie? We wore earphones and listened to a cassette-tape tour in the Guggenheim, had lunch at a funky little place in the Village, and took in an off-Broadway play in the late afternoon. And we had time just to walk, look in windows, watch people, and talk. We talked all the day long . . . about us, about our future, about our feelings. I'm so afraid I'm going to wake up from this dream. You know, I can't decide if it is Jake's near brush with death or his decision to terminate analysis, or both, that have made these changes in him. Or maybe it's just all tied up together in some way that is not clear to me right now. Last night he came home from school and went right out to play tennis, even though I had dinner all ready. So I guess things aren't so different after all. Only difference is I don't care so much anymore. "Do what you want," I say silently to myself, "and I shall do what I want, too."

It seems that this is a time of change for everyone. Timothy came over to tell me that he got into ortho school (orthodontics—offered only to the best of dentists), and he introduced me to a medical student, Denny, who is taking over the lease on the apartment next door in June. Denny is a very reluctant future doctor—apparently doesn't want to follow in his father's footsteps. I talked to him for two and a half hours, long past the time that Timothy finished his coffee and left. So Denny may be dropping out of medical school. And Evelyn is definitely pregnant and staying that way, so she and Michael are making plans. And Nancy and Adam were just offered jobs. Adam will teach at Yale; I knew he'd land some wonderful position. From now on he'll probably publish a book a year. And Nancy—Nancy and I talked last week; we talked all day about her job offer, from a university in Oregon, a long way from here. She also discussed it in group therapy, and they all urged her to go, to take the job. The problem is leaving Brook, of course, because he can't move out there with her. It is a *very* good opportunity; she'd be teaching only one composition course, and two advanced specialty courses in her area of expertise—and possible tenure track too! I don't know yet if she can do it, however. She adores Brook, even if he doesn't want to have children with her.

So everyone is going through changes, and sometimes I wonder what it will be like not to be involved in these lives anymore, except by letter or phone—and surely that will grow less and less frequent, as such things do. I'm leaving all this familiarity—the university, my friends, even this miserable apartment, and you. It will be just me and Jake and Bonnie there on the cable cars of San Francisco. Must we expect backsliding there, I wonder?

Sincerely,
JEANNE

May 5

DEAR DR. FRICKMAN,

The pressure is on for Jake—studying for exams and boards and preparing to leave school after so many years. Between his studying and his relaxation time (playing tennis), we don't see him much. But it's OK; I mean, I know this is a difficult time for him, and anyway, I'm very busy with my own world. We will have a lot of time together when this is all over. Did Jake tell you he's entered a tennis tournament over at Elkins Park? Nothing like being a glutton for pressure; I do believe he loves to test his own limits as much as he likes to test mine. He doesn't usually get too far in these tournaments, so it shouldn't take that much time away from study-ing.

My brother and his wife and two babies arrived from Boston yesterday to spend three days with us. I can't tell how Jake feels about this; perhaps he's told you. But we just wanted to get together once more before we move next month. (Next month! My God!) I haven't spent this much time with my brother in years. I see him so differently now, I can hardly get over it. Somehow, I guess, it's that he's neither my great, idolized big brother nor the teasing, privileged ogre that he use to be to me. He's another person, a separate person toward whom I feel some warmth, love, a person who has his own different life, his own different yet similar prob-lems and joys. This probably sounds mundane, but I can't express what a surprise it is to me. And his wife, my sister-in-law, she's so obviously able to "take care" of him, to put up with his ego, to support him and admire him while remaining content with her own situation. I'm in awe. Bonnie loves the company of her two big cousins (eighteen months and three years old); I feel rather sad that they will not grow up knowing each other well. Now I can't get to reknow my brother, whom I actually like after all this time. And I think I could be very close to my sister-in-law if I saw her more often; our lives are very different, but I have the feeling I could learn so much from her.

This leave-taking process is an interesting one. I've written postcards to some old friends to let them know we're moving West. Today I received letters from two friends—one woman I went to college with and one I went to the first year of graduate school with. One has recently had her second child, is fifty pounds overweight (oh, how she used to be careful about her figure!) and sounds iso-lated, bored, and depressed. The other has one baby, only four months old, and is getting a divorce and taking a full-time position as a textbook editor with a publishing firm. As I read the letters I found I could empathize with both friends, with the financial and emotional entrapment of one, and with the financial precariousness and the struggle to be emotionally free of the other. Empathy with the conflict of being the everpresent mother, on the one hand, and of being otherwise fulfilled while being a half-absent mother on the other. I see myself somewhere between their two worlds—unable either to remain at home as constant care-giver, or to leave home and give up that care to someone else despite the possibilities for other satisfactions and goals. Now that Bonnie is able to creep around the floor and wriggle out of my arms to be on her own, I find myself day-dreaming about having another child. Good God, what power has this life force, this urge to procreate—power beyond all reasonable intelligence, I think!

Now I look, on the other hand, at my brother and at Jake, whose lives go on much the same whether they have none or one or two or more children. Oh, they give up some nights out when there is no baby-sitter, and they hear more noise when they arrive home for supper, and they have more financial responsibility as providers, but they can't begin to know the personal conflict, the difficulty of combining the wishes to be a supermother and an independent person with some other accomplishment as well.

Oh, and neither do you, I'm afraid. Just because you're a psychiatrist, doesn't mean you understand a woman's position. Your wife probably feels the same way I do.

Give her my best.

JEANNE

May 12

DEAR DR. FRICKMAN,

Sometimes I imagine my letters to you (a defined but anonymous and silent audience) as newspaper articles, sometimes feature articles, sometimes more trivial, "filler" material, sometimes in the category of classified ads—even like those little Thank You St. Jude classifieds—you know, "Thank you St. Jude for blessings given so abundantly." I always wonder if those little ads are a code to a hit man or something like that. Or perhaps my writings might fall more to the editorial page because they are not exactly neutral reporting.

Anyway! Today I have banner headlines: "My heart leaps up," or any other poetic line you can think of. My grant application has been accepted and I've been awarded a generous one-year grant, including travel money, to write my book on mother-artists! Do you see how wonderful this is? Do you understand how much this means? I can have my own money, at least for awhile; I don't have to leave Bonnie for extended periods of time each day; I can travel wherever my research takes me (within limits of course); and I can study subjects I'm extremely interested in—women and mother-hood and creativity. Direct interviewing, research into women who have managed to do both (be mothers *and* artists) in times long before women's liberation, and research in psychological theory about women's creativity—all of these will be part of this exciting work! I received the letter just yesterday so you must forgive me if I'm still bubbling like a veritable fountain. You know, I think Jake is even genuinely happy for me, and we're already making plans for some vacation time together in England after I've done some re-search and interviewing there—probably in the fall.

Also exciting was the fact that Jake won his tennis tournament this weekend (as you no doubt have heard), an event far more excit-ing than an outsider might realize. I am *convinced* that Jake's tennis playing, the actual physical game, is little better than when he had played in any other tournament. This one was different because of his *mind*, because he has so suddenly (now why does it seem sudden after all this long, long time?) become somehow so different. I could swear it's just been in the time since we've decided to move. At any rate, that shiny trophy sitting there on our telephone-spool table is at least half yours, I figure.

Nancy and Adam are taking me out to lunch today to celebrate my good news; Evelyn offered to baby-sit for Bonnie, so I feel free as a breeze, or more like I'm floating in the breeze. I have to close this letter now so I can write a note to Randy in London. He'll be excited to hear this news too.

Congratulations, by the way, on the tennis tournament.

Best,
JEANNE

May 20

DEAR DR. FRICKMAN,

Again, again I've been lying awake wondering if we should really be moving away, leaving you. I mean, you've become such an integral part of us, of our marriage even, and I'm afraid of what might happen when we're three thousand miles away.

Maybe this is too sudden; we need a longer time. It's like Bonnie and me. She's not ready to be weaned from the breast yet; she's certainly cut down on nursing now that she can drink from a cup and eat real food, but she still wants to nurse early in the morning and at bedtime. Who would want to take that comfort away from her when she's doing so beautifully, growing, learning, smiling to catch us and include us within her world? She will give up nursing when she's ready, all in good time; there's no rushing such things. Then why are we, grown-ups all—at least we pretend to be—why are we making this sudden break from this other vital, symbiotic relationship?

Is this all my own fantasy? Unrealistic fear? I can't for the life of me get Jake to talk about it, not even when I get up like this at three in the morning after tossing for over an hour. I feel like I have been climbing a long, long ladder out of a deep hole, and now, just after I have clutched the top and peeked over to the beautiful world outside, someone has kicked the ladder out from under me and my hold on the rim is precarious indeed. What really scares me is that I might have kicked the ladder away myself.

Good Lord, such visions at 3:00 A.M. are not going to help me get back to sleep. Let me talk to us both about happier things. Let's see. Evelyn and Michael are to be married in three weeks; they are very much in love and extremely excited about expecting a baby. Evelyn is still working on her graduate studies but medieval history and alchemy have certainly been moved down on the scale of values to make room for current events and new roles. It's hard to believe this all started at that little party—how long ago was it? It seems very long ago.

What else? Ah yes. I've finished teaching for the semester except for giving and grading the final exam and getting grades in. And on Friday I will get dressed up and go to school for my oral examination on my dissertation, basically a formality, and then celebrate at the faculty club with my dissertation committee and the department chairman. As soon as all of that is over, I'll begin getting things organized for our move to San Francisco. Ah, what *do* you think of this move, I'd like to know. Is this a healthy move? Is it OK? What do *you* feel about it? It's just not right, somehow, that your feelings are unknown; unshared, I mean. You must have become somewhat involved in Jake's life. In our lives. And now suddenly, the relationship is over. It's inhuman, it's artificial, it's cold. I'm tired. Good morning.

JEANNE

May 29

DEAR DR. FRICKMAN,

Oh, it's going to be OK. This is just a note to tell you not to worry (if indeed I might flatter myself enough to think that you might). Jake will be OK, and I will be OK, and we will be OK. I guess moving away just has to have its mourning side and its rites to help one make the transition. Jake, my dear wonderful Jake, asked me what I'd like for my twenty-seventh birthday and suggested we ask some friends to go out to dinner with us to celebrate as well as to say good-bye. So—David and Pamela, Timothy and Holly, Michael and Evelyn, Nancy and Brook, Sydney and Mandy, Adam and Alice, Sara and her new boyfriend Dick, and two other women (from my book group) and their husbands all joined us for dinner at Zorba the Greek's downtown. We took up nearly the whole place and stayed for hours. I shall like to remember them all with the rhythms of Greek dance music going through my head. And somehow, it made me feel readier to go, to leave. We shall make new friends; it will take a while, but there will be new, interesting people to reach out to once again in California, people to love, to depend on, to be interdependent with. Nancy is definitely leaving Brook to go to Oregon—and that means we'll be living relatively close to each other. I do admire her courage in leaving.

Jake will soon have boards over with and then we just have graduations and Michael and Evelyn's wedding, and then packing up and renting a truck and then we're off. So—in case there is a human being inside of that analytic skin, rest assured that we'll make it OK without you!

Sincerely,
JEANNE

June 6

DEAR DR. FRICKMAN,

All my favorite dentists—David, Timothy, Michael—received their D.D.S. degrees on Thursday. Yesterday morning I received my Ph.D.—a wonderful feeling of accomplishment. But I couldn't help comparing it to Bonnie, and it's only an attractive bit of printed paper compared to the delight of my life, an ongoing challenge, life itself. Don't get me wrong. I'm not saying women are to be totally fulfilled by the creative processes of their own bodies. I am happy to have both the degree and my daughter, though I have the feeling that this situation has a lot of built-in conflicts that might be avoided by opting for only one or the other. Anyway, back to the present: Jake received his M.D. yesterday afternoon, and since all our available relatives were there—my parents, his mother, his sister, his aunt and uncle—we had a party afterwards in the midst of boxes and piles of books in our half-packed apartment.

And then today we went to Evelyn and Michael's wedding and reception. They were married in the chapel down near the university. I actually cried. I think the prospect of moving has put me into an extremely vulnerable state; I am up and down almost without reason. At the reception we sat with David and Pamela and Timothy and Allison (his latest). David got into one of his cynical-sarcastic moods and questioned Jake about analysis and about terminating analysis, kind of teasing him about it. Jake didn't really seem to mind and pretty much laughed it off, but I was incensed! So I found myself defending Jake and the process of analysis—all quite unasked for, of course. I must be out of my mind. Surely I've not become a believer, do you think?

But Jake has grown a lot, hasn't he? I'm just worried—still—about making this transition. I mean, what if he needs to talk to you three weeks from now and we're three thousand miles away? This —starting tomorrow—is his very last week with you. And in a few days after that, we'll be off in our rental truck, like the early settlers who packed everything up in covered wagons and rode west. Of course they didn't have Egg McMuffins or Big Macs to look forward to on the way. This has been *such* a busy weekend, and I begin packing seriously in the morning—so good night. I'll write again before we leave.

Sincerely,
JEANNE

June 13

DEAR DR. FRICKMAN,

This is my last letter. We're on the road as I write—in a motel in Kansas City for the night, quite far away from you, indeed from everything familiar. Bonnie is sound asleep, and Jake is falling asleep watching an old Clint Eastwood movie. I didn't have one second of time to write during the past week. Only now do I feel as though we've finally escaped the whirlwind—so many last-minute details and good-byes. You know, I still feel somewhat cheated when I think that I never got to meet you; it might bother me forever.

Well, this is really it, Dr. Frickman; I'm not sure I believe it yet. What, I wonder, is this like for *you?* What must you feel like after listening to my Jake an hour a day, five days a week for two and a half years, listening to him tell about his most intimate thoughts and feelings? You and your damnable "austere code of the psychoanalyst." Big words that are the walls you hide behind, supposedly in service of the patient—but also, I suspect, to protect you from being vulnerable yourself, a shell around a turtle. But I refuse to believe that you do this easily; you *must* feel the break too. Or is that just the fantasy of every analysand—or in this case, the analysand's wife? And how about me, my letters I mean? I wonder if you will miss receiving them . . . my complaints, my worries, sometimes my gratitude. What will it be like for you to lose touch with us after such intimate communications? After all, you have been hidden in your "analytic incognito" and, for me at least, you are really almost totally an imaginary figure, a fantasy, a phantom, an unreal combination of a myriad of people I have known. And even to Jake you are not truly a person, I think. But to you, Jake—and me, too, I imagine—are much more real, so it should be you who should have to go through some kind of mourning at such a loss. Or have I got it all wrong? Are you truly not involved, and perhaps rather glad to be finished with a patient (and his letter-writing partner)? As usual, I shall receive no answer to such wonderings. Mystery for life.

Jake and I have been talking about my plans for writing the book on mother-artists. As it stands right now, Bonnie and I will fly to London for six weeks in September, and Jake will take two weeks off and join us to travel around a bit in October. I received a letter from Randy just before we left. He has finished a new book of poems, to be published this winter. He is also full of plans to show me around London—bookstores and Bloomsbury and the home where Yeats and, later, Sylvia Plath and her two children lived. And he will introduce me to some friends and we will go out to Stratford to see some Shakespearean plays, and visit Oxford and Cambridge and attend several concerts. He has talked to his landlady about baby-sitting for Bonnie when I have to go to the library or out at night—I plan to carry her around most of the time. Or perhaps she'll be walking a bit on her own, almost a year old by then! Oh to be in England now that spring is here.

And now what does one say? How does one say good-bye to someone one doesn't know and yet has been so intimately involved with? Well, I leave you with the dream I had the night before we left—for whatever it may be worth: I was in a huge, high, empty room, the walls of which were covered with mirrors, as in an amusement park. I was alone in the room, growing frantic to find the way out, but I had this intense feeling that I wasn't quite alone, that there was a shadow in the mirrors. Each time I tried to catch sight of it, however, it seemed to flit to another mirror. Somewhere in the haze that seems so clear while one is dreaming, I began to know the shadow was you—and that you were trying to help me find the way out. When I realized this, I spoke out loud and said, "No, thanks," and sat down on a sofa (which I hadn't seen earlier) and began to read a book. That's all. That's absolutely all.

TV's Clint Eastwood is shooting the bad guys, but my own wild-west rider is sound asleep and I must sleep now too. How could this be my last letter to you? I'm hooked, and I'll be writing to you from time to time from the city of cable cars. Drop us a line if you get a chance.

Sincerely,
JEANNE

July 15

DEAR DR. FRICKMAN,

San Francisco is glorious! We rented a charming, small house with blue shutters near the top of a steep hill, and Bonnie and Jake and I take walking tours whenever we can. Jake is quite busy with internship, but I use the nights when he's working to do my own work on my book, which is going well, I think.

Bonnie and I go to the Y two mornings a week for Bonnie's swimming lessons; we both go in the pool with a great bunch of other women and babies, and we sing songs and play games to help our little ones feel comfortable in the water. Through this activity I've met several nice women, mothers, and it has opened a whole new world to be able to talk to other people who have children. One woman has an advanced degree in anthropology and plans to go back to teach in college when her children are of school age (she has two). We're becoming good friends, so I'm beginning to feel that this is really home.

Jake too seems to be settling in OK, and he is often home for breakfast since he does not have to meet with you at some ungodly hour of the morning! And you know, he does truly talk to me more. I think our relationship is growing, that we are working towards a deeper intimacy. And I do give you credit, Dr. Frickman, I really do.

Do I sound like everything's coming up roses? Yes, I suppose I must. And you know, of course, that life is not actually like that. Life has its highs and lows; indeed, the geography of this city is a constant reminder. But I've decided that climbing up from the valleys need not be like pushing a bicycle (or a stroller) up a steep hill. There are mechanical means to help one—like the cable cars here in the city which can smooth things out considerably. And so . . . that is why I've seen a psychoanalyst here in San Francisco and have made plans to begin my own analysis when I get back from England in October. Perhaps you are not at all surprised. . . . I think I'm more surprised than anyone could be. Of course, now I shall not be writing to you any longer; I wouldn't want anything to interfere with my analysis. You understand.

So—here's to the time when we all meet and all mysteries are revealed on that great couch in the sky. Farewell, Dr. Frickman, farewell.

With love,
JEANNE DANIELS